MAVERICKS:
DOC GRIMSON'S OUTLAW POSSE

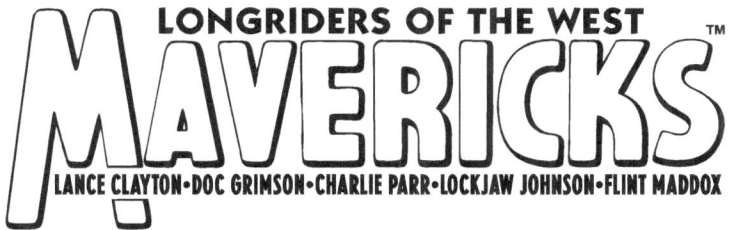

LONGRIDERS OF THE WEST™
MAVERICKS

LANCE CLAYTON•DOC GRIMSON•CHARLIE PARR•LOCKJAW JOHNSON•FLINT MADDOX

DOC GRIMSON'S OUTLAW POSSE

By Kent Thorn

POPULAR PUBLICATIONS • 2018

PUBLISHING HISTORY

"Doc Grimson's Outlaw Posse" originally appeared in the December 1934 issue of
  Mavericks magazine (Vol. 1, No. 4). Copyright 1934, 1961 by Popular Publications,
  Inc. All Rights Reserved.

CHAPTER 1
MAVERICK GUNMEN

CHARLIE PARR stiffened in his saddle. His sharp blue eyes narrowed through the distance ahead on a tiny dark blot which he had picked out along the trail, from a height of ground half a mile back. That minute interruption on the trail side, where the sage and manzanita gave way to rocks and barren ground, would have meant nothing to most men, but to the white-mustached, keen-eyed Charlie Parr, it meant a great deal. It meant gunplay certainly; perhaps a killing.

Beside him four other riders reined in, staring, crinkle-eyed, in the same direction. Charlie turned his weather-tanned features toward Doc Grimson at his side. "Two bodies there, Doc," he said gruffly. "Can't tell just where they was shot from here, but they're hurt bad. Thought I seen 'em wiggle a mite just then—"

But already Doc was spurring ahead toward their grim goal. Behind him, crowding the turns of the down-grade, pounding up great clouds of dust, rode the four other Mavericks. And it took only a few minutes of that swift pace for them all to see, flung out on the rock just ahead, the forms of two men—one a rancher, to judge from his close-cropped gray mustache and his clothes; the other, perhaps, his foreman. Only now, whether or not they had actually moved as Charlie had thought, they were very still. They would never move again.

Doc Grimson flung himself from the saddle and knelt beside the two bodies. For a split second he hesitated, eyes flaring as he took in the significance of the sign scrawled in the dust between the sprawling figures. But the hesitation was almost imperceptible. Doc was first of all a physician. Wordless, he turned his attention to an examination of the men themselves.

Not so the others. They had dismounted behind him and were staring at the crude but damning mark which had briefly caught his attention. It was plain enough to them—that representation of a slick ear, with the numeral five before it.

"The Five Mavericks!" Lance Clayton exclaimed between suddenly set teeth. He said no more than that, but his eyes were blue pools of anger and unconsciously his hands lifted over the butts of the twin six-guns which hung low on either thigh.

Flint Maddox began to curse in a low, vicious voice, steadily. It was blasting profanity, meaningless except for the rage which backed up in his throat and hoarsened his voice.

Lockjaw Johnson's long face flushed. He said, "If I ever git my hands on them pole-cats I'm goin' to twist every bone in their bodies until it breaks!"

Only Charlie Parr, white-mustached, his face like a wrinkled mask of leather, was silent. But his wiry, spidery figure was tense and his ageless blue eyes were bleak as winter skies.

Doc Grimson got up, dusting off his knees absently. The set of his mouth was bitter. "Shot square in the back, each of 'em!" he announced. "They're still warm, though. Couldn't have been killed more than fifteen minutes ago. If we'd been a little earlier, we'd have heard the shots."

"Murdered like dogs," Lance Clayton said, "and our sign between them!"

"What was they shot with, Doc?" Charlie Parr asked.

"Winchesters, I think," Doc told him briefly.

"The killers can't be far," Flint Maddox flung out, his voice still shaking with the rage. "Let's get after them!" As he spoke, he turned, reaching for the reins of his ground-tied mount.

Good cause had the Mavericks to have that slick-ear sign burned into their minds with an acid bitterness. Rumors of brutal crimes—later backed up by actual murder and robberies—had come to them and brought the inseparable Five riding, grim and determined, from one of their mountain hideouts to expose the ruthless killers and to clear a reputation of which they were proud.

Not one of the Five had ever killed a man excepting in open warfare. Whenever they carried through a robbery or threw in their guns on the side of the underdog in any range trouble, the affair went off without injury to ordinary, decent citizens. But these two men had been shot in the back, killed without a chance, most likely. And there, for all to see, was the signature of the Mavericks, the damning murder brand, already dyed scarlet by the victims' blood.

CHARLIE PARR shook his head. "We can try cuttin' for sign," he said. "But it won't be any use."

"Why?" Flint snapped. "They couldn't have flown!"

Charlie Parr pointed to the ground in front of them. "They knew what they were doin'," he said. "They come down off those rocks there, two of 'em, on foot. They must have shot from that

3

clump of manzanita above the trail. It's the best place. They could have had their broncs tied down in the ravine the other side of the ridge. Then they come down here, turned the bodies over and went through the pockets—you can see that. When they'd got through, they rubbed out their sign enough to keep anybody from reckernizin' the boot tracks—they only had a few steps to go to git back to the rocks—walked back to their broncs and rode off. Jaspers that would do it that way ain't goin' to leave sign in a country where there ain't anything easier than to cover a trail. I bet them broncs ain't even shod. Take 'em over rocks an' we couldn't even find the marks that a horseshoe'll make. No. We can cut for sign but we won't find any."

Flint hesitated. It was plain that his anger still urged immediate action—plain, also, that he knew that when Charlie talked of sign he was worth listening to. "What in hell are we supposed to do, then," he grated, "let 'em get clean away after we've ridden through seven counties to get to 'em?"

Doc Grimson said quietly, "We aren't through yet. We haven't even started."

Lance Clayton lifted his head suddenly, his keen ear the first to catch what the others heard a split second later—the faint thud of hoof-beats in the pines on the left of the trail. A moment later a rider appeared, pushing through the bushes which bordered the woods the other side of the trail. The rider was a girl.

The group had whirled, alert. Now they relaxed imperceptibly. They had only time to see that she was a remarkably pretty girl before she pulled up with an exclamation and slipped from the saddle. Her eyes were riveted on the two bodies.

"What—what has happened?" she asked, the soft color fading from her face. Then she went forward with a little rush. "Uncle Fred!" she cried, horrified, and knelt beside the elderly man who looked like a ranchman. "Oh! He's dead! Somebody shot him. It's—it's *murder!*"

Instinctively she shrank back. Then her eyes fell on the sign, blood-scrawled in the dust. For an instant she stared at it, paralyzed, stiffened lips forming the words, "The Five Mavericks!"

She got slowly to her feet, wide hazel eyes turning toward the men behind her. Her mouth opened to speak and then for the first time, apparently, she realized that there were just five of them, and for the first time fear joined the horror in her gaze.

"You—*you* are the Five Mavericks," she gasped, her hands going to her throat. "You murdered them!"

Doc Grimson asked quietly. "Do we look like murderers, ma'am?"

She disregarded him. Her eyes traveled in fascinated recognition from one to the other. There was fear in them still, but there was also the beginning of righteous anger.

"You're the man they call Doc Grimson," she said to the slender, grave figure who had spoken to her. "And that's Charlie Parr—and Lance Clayton—and Johnson—and Flint Maddox. I recognize you all from your descriptions. You'll hang for this, you—you beasts! Do you hear—you'll hang for it!"

Charlie Parr said, "We're the Five Mavericks, all right, ma'am, but we didn't murder your uncle or this other feller."

"We don't shoot men in the back," said Lance Clayton, his blue eyes smoldering.

The girl's anger had gotten the better of her fear now. "And I suppose you didn't shoot the guard and the driver of the Mule Corners stage from ambush!" she blazed out at them. "I suppose you didn't murder the cashier of the bank at Cantada and two innocent men who happened to be in the bank, one of them unarmed!"

"No," said Doc Grimson gravely, "we didn't. And we didn't blow up the two mail clerks of the Denver Express with dynamite, either—or do any of the other little tricks that the brand of the Five Mavericks has been signed to. We've ridden a long way to find out who's impersonating us, and when we do find out, somebody's goin' to be middlin' sorry for it."

The girl said scornfully, "Do you expect anybody to swallow that—when I've caught you here, red-handed?"

"No—and nobody will," a harsh voice crackled suddenly from the underbrush nearby. "Get 'em high, hombres—quick!" AT THE first words, the Five Mavericks whirled—to find themselves looking into the grim muzzles of a pair of six-shooters.

"My boys have got you covered from the bushes," the man who held them warned. "Don't try anything funny, unless you want a sudden ticket to hell!"

He was a youngish man, cold-eyed, with a jaw carved out of granite, and his mouth, at this moment, appeared to be no more than a slit. On his ornate beaded vest a sheriff's star shone in the morning sun with malevolent glitter.

Doc Grimson let his half-drawn Colts slip unobtrusively back into their holsters. He had started his draw as he had whirled at the lawman's first word, but even the fastest draw cannot be made before a slow man's finger can tighten on a trigger, and Doc's lightning movement had been arrested midway.

Now, he said easily, "That's an old trick—the men in the bushes business. But it isn't necessary, Sheriff. We're here to help the law, not to fight it."

"Don't make any mistake, you skunk," the sheriff told him savagely. "My men are there, and the law can help itself. I've got you, *and that's all I need.*"

As he spoke, as though to confirm his words, the barrel of a Winchester protruded visibly from the bushes from which he had come, and to the left of that the brush stirred and a voice said, "Why warn 'em, Sheriff? We wouldn't ask nothin' better than a chance to smoke 'em down like they smoked these two pore fellers!"

"Shootin's too good for this gang," the lawman said, his eyes suddenly cruel. "I'm aimin' to see 'em dance on air, with all the fixin's. Turn your backs, you. Ben, you collect their artillery. Grif, you fan 'em for hideout guns."

Doc Grimson shrugged and turned his back as directed. The others did likewise. One man could scarcely have kept the drop on that Five, but others, hidden in the brush, made a different story. There was nothing to do but give in.

"Comes of losin' our tempers," Charlie Parr commented

bitterly. "Next thing we know, we'll be lettin' a herd of cattle slip up on us an' tromp us to death."

"Next thing you know," the sheriff told him, with a note of triumph in his voice, "you won't know nothin'. Your trial is goin' to be prompt and pronto, you murderin' bushwhackers! You're goin' to stretch hemp so fast you'll still be kickin' when you get to the other side."

"If you git a trial at all, you'll be lucky," one of the other men observed sardonically. "My reckonin' is that there ain't no jail strong enough to keep you safe when folks hear you've been caught up with."

"Tie their hands behind 'em," the sheriff directed. "We'll take no chances with these varmints."

"You're making a mistake, Sheriff," Doc Grimson told him. "The men you want—"

"—Are the men I've got," the lawman interrupted. "Shut your mouth, or I'll shut it for you!"

Lance Clayton, his hands tied behind his back, looked at the sheriff with eyes suddenly dangerous. "You talk big, hombre," he said, "to men who have their hands tied up. Better be careful—we've got loose from tighter places than this."

The sheriff's eyes were cold sinks of malevolence. "When you get out of this one," he said, "you'll be dead."

The malicious triumph in his eyes puzzled Lance. He didn't look like just a lawman who had trapped some wanted men. He looked like a man who had some secret, hating pleasure in it—some motive entirely apart from the natural satisfaction of a lawman who has made a good capture.

Something of the same repressed exultation was reflected on the faces of the other four men with the sheriff. Lance realized suddenly that they made five also, and suspicion plucked faintly at his mind. There were five men who impersonated them. Could this five be…? It was odd that they should turn up at this very spot so quickly and so quietly. But he realized with a twinge of disappointment that there was no real evidence for his suspicions.

Working quietly at his bonds behind his back, Lance tried to remember the details of the crimes which had recently been committed under the sign of the slick ear and the numeral five. Had the men been individually described as looking like the real Mavericks? The five in the sheriff's party could not be the ones, in that case. But after all, that was no evidence, either. The outlaws who were impersonating the Mavericks had been masked in every case and no one, in the excitement, would have gotten a calm look at them. People always saw what they expected to see. No doubt there would be dozens ready to swear in all good faith that the actual robbers were like the real Mavericks in every detail.

His hands were nearly free by now—would have been free long ago had it not been necessary to work at the bonds under that lawman's frozen and watchful eye. He wondered if Doc and the rest were nearly ready. It would be better to make their break before the fifth man got back with the horses. But Charlie Parr would probably take a long time to get free, and Lockjaw was always slow as molasses. So there would be only three of them to go up against five heavily armed men. Three—against odds that spelled death any way you looked at it.

TYING UP the Five Mavericks was always a more or less useless proceeding. They knew the trick of holding wristbones and muscles so that the ropes could not really be drawn tight. It was a wonder that this sheriff had not heard of that fact, since he and everybody else, had apparently heard so much about them.

There were, in truth, few spots between the Canadian Line and Mexico City where men did not talk of the quintette, and of their exploits along their peculiar branch of the Owlhoot Trail. But though they were cursed by sheriffs and the law-abiding with automatic vehemence, an acute ear might have detected a certain lack of heartiness in the cursing. For the Five Mavericks were outlaws of a special brand.

They were just as apt to prey on other riders of the dim trails as they were to plunder the over-rich and ruthless among the smugly respectable. And many an honest man who had been down and out, and many a decent rancher in trouble, had as much reason to bless their names as the other sort had to curse them. It was only here, in Bear Creek County, that ordinary citizens cursed them with conviction and a sincere desire to see them stretch rope—Bear Creek County, whither they had come to wipe out the blood-blotch which murdering impostors had cast upon their name.

Charlie Parr, the old-timer of the quintette, had gone it alone, with Lockjaw Johnson, along the Owlhoot Trail largely because he could not stand unnecessary killing. He had been a member of Boot Hill Kennedy's gang until the latter's ruthlessness disgusted him. An argument over that point resulted fatally to Boot Hill and Charlie for a short time became leader of the gang. He was deposed bloodlessly when, during the course of a bank robbery, the cashier's wife, happening on the affair by accident, spread her arms before the safe and said that she would be killed before she allowed them to loot it. It would have been easy to move her aside, but Charlie Parr forbade the gang to touch her. Only Lockjaw Johnson followed him after that— Lockjaw, who was too dumb to understand any of the fine points of the argument but who had a loyalty to Charlie which would have carried him to the backlog of hell and back had the older man given the word.

Lance Clayton, young, big-shouldered, buoyant, was outside the law because a lady had once confided to him her money troubles. Lance, broke, held up a saloon for her benefit, turned the money over to her (she subsequently publicly branded as a thief and disowned him privately) and escaped arrest by virtue of good nerves and a fast horse.

Flint Maddox, hard-fisted, melancholy-eyed and honest as the day is long, had once been a prosperous rancher. Ruined by the ruthless greed of a neighboring land-hog, he had lost his wife and children in an incendiary fire. Morally certain that his enemy was responsible for this last tragedy but unable to prove it, he had killed the stockman and his foreman in a saloon fight and left town two jumps ahead of a crooked sheriff who wanted to frame him for murder. As was the case with Lance Clayton, the gang headed by Doc Grimson and Charlie Parr offered him

11

the only kind of outlaw life to which he could have reconciled his principles.

Of the Five, Doc Grimson was the man of mystery. East-erner, gambler, educated man, and a physician of extraordinary skill, he had never told even his companions why he had for-saken a brilliant future to come West to live outside the law. Of him they knew only that he was a man of many parts and endless ingenuity, a sure friend to his friends and sudden death to his enemies, by virtue of gun-hands that moved with the lightning, flickering speed of a rattler's tongue.

Watching him now, Lance sensed by Doc's immobility that his hands must be free. He wondered whether or not Flint, too, was ready.

The man who had gone for the horses was coming back with them. Maybe it would be better to wait until he had gotten there, for there would be some confusion as the group got ready to mount. Just now, one of the sheriff's posse—a young, straight-looking boy who formed the greatest objection to Lance's half-formed suspicion that these men were the impos-tors—was standing apart, talking to the girl. Something would have to be done to get him in closer.

Doc said suddenly, "Are we going to stand here all day? Let's have a little action." His words were addressed to the sheriff, but there was an intonation in them that told the others he was ready.

Flint Maddox said, "Yeah, I'm ready to do a little movin' myself."

"You skunks are liable to do your next movin' up and down,"

the sheriff cut in with cold significance. "Don't be in too much of a hurry for it."

Lance stared at him contemptuously. "You bat-eared, frog-eyed pole-cat," he said deliberately, "what do you mean by callin' decent gents skunks? You was too yeller to do it before we was tied up. Come over here and I'll push a boot heel through your white-livered middle!"

The lawman looked at him through eyes that were mere venomous slits, but said nothing.

Lance, thought. "I've got to get him over here some way."

Lockjaw cut in, blandly unaware of his purpose. "That's talkin', Lance," he applauded. "We've took too much already off this belly-crawlin' tin-star. Spit in his eye!"

Lance walked toward the lawman. "You haven't got the nerve to hit me," he jeered. "You're too scared I might get loose sometime and remember about it. You're yeller all the way through!"

One of the men at the sheriff's side, seeing Lockjaw closing in with Lance, put his hand on the butt of his holstered gun.

"Keep back, you fool," the sheriff warned sharply, "or I'll—"

He never finished. Lance's right fist whipped around and landed flush on the point of his jaw. The lawman's head snapped back; his knees sagged. A Colt exploded violently as the man at his side drew and fired. But Lance, moving with the swift precision of a machine, had stepped in and sidewise, catching the sheriff as he tottered drunkenly, and using the dazed lawman's body as a shield. The bullet missed, but nipped at Lance's moving shoulder, ripping cloth.

LOCKJAW, HIS hand still bound, left the ground like a catapult, both feet driving for the stomach of the man with the gun. The latter went down backwards; doubled up with a great agonized grunt, while the hurtling Maverick hit the ground on the back of his neck. The force of the fall would have broken any head but Lockjaw's.

Doc Grimson's hand flashed down too fast to see and came up with a rock. Cat-like, he rushed, angling sideways against the drawn gun of the third man of the posse, and heaved the jagged rock with all the snap of his broad shoulder behind it. Beautifully timed, the missile smacked into the man's face. It hit just as the posseman's thumb released the hammer of the gun which was pointing at the darting figure of Doc before him. The shot went wide. Almost simultaneously Doc drove at the gunman's right arm, disregarding the hand which held the Colt. Doc's left struck hard and sure for the hollow of the other elbow, while his right slipped between arm and body, circling up behind the shoulder. The posseman shrieked in sudden agony as the shoulder cartilage tore and the bone threatened to go. His right hand dropped the gun, as he came up on his toes, seeking to ease the pressure of that relentless grip.

Flint Maddox, whose rush had been a split second behind Doc's, caught up the fallen gun and trained it on the man who had been leading the horses.

That individual had stopped in astonishment, going for his Colt so late that he dared not fire into the milling mêlée which Lance's sudden move had brought on.

Lance's right hand had dived now for the six-gun of the

unconscious sheriff, still held as a shield, and the weapon came up like a blued flash. His voice cracked out, "Drop your guns, you two—I don't want to kill you!"

The clean-looking youngster who had been talking to the girl had drawn and rushed forward, seeking a chance to fire without risking his comrades. At Lance's words, he checked an instant, but then, with set teeth, rushed in, six-shooter steady, disregarding the gun which menaced him. Lance lifted the barrel of his Colt and prepared to bring it down on the youngster's head.

Suddenly Doc's arm licked out, like a striking snake, and caught the young deputy's gun-wrist, twisting it and pulling it at the same time. Doc Grimson, seeing the rush at Lance, had dropped the disabled sheriff and had shot for the youngster. Over-balanced, the kid badge-toter came to his knees, his gun suddenly in Doc's magic fingers.

That ended it. So rapid had been the action that the man with the horses was still trying to decide whom to shoot at or whether to shoot at all. Now, with three guns trained on him, he dropped his Colt and came forward with his hands over his head.

Charlie Parr had not even left his place. His wrists were too thin and his hands too gnarled to enable him to get loose from a rope easily, and he had evidently seen no use for such calisthenics as Lockjaw's. He stood at ease, face calm, blue eyes beginning to twinkle with humor now above the laconic droop of his flowing white mustache.

"Nice work, boys," he remarked. "Lockjaw, you didn't break your danged head, did you?"

Lockjaw twisted his neck around to look back at him. "Not none," he said, "but if I ever git my hands loose, I'm shore gonna be rubbin' it some!"

Charlie said, placidly, "Better cut him loose, Doc, an' me, too. From the way the young lady has been lookin' over her shoulder at the ridge there, I judge some fellers might come surgin' over here any minute. We better ride."

CHAPTER 2
POSSE MEAT

LANCE DROPPED the sheriff, got out his knife and cut the ropes which bound Lockjaw, while Flint performed a similar service for Charlie Parr.

Lockjaw got to his feet, rubbing his head, and grinning at the lawman he had assaulted. That individual was regaining breath and consciousness simultaneously and he looked both unhappy and bewildered.

"Amigo," Lockjaw told him, "when you and me tangle it's kind of hard to know who gits the worst of it."

The sheriff sat up, shaking his head dazedly. Then memory apparently came to him and he got to his feet, cursing viciously.

"Shucks!" Lance addressed him. "Is that pretty—sayin' language like that before a lady? And you in that pretty vest and everything!"

16

"Looks to me," said Lockjaw, eyeing the garment with admiration, "like he don't hardly deserve a vest like that. Now me, I'd look mighty well in them beads." He began to sidle toward the lawman. "Whoa! whoa!" he said soothingly, "now you just stand right still and don't get excited, while I borry that vest of yourn. Keep ca'm and don't move—but especially, don't move, because I never did have no love for sheriffs and I'd shore be apt to tromple your ears right down."

There was pure killer in the sheriff's eyes as he shrugged out of the vest and flung it down on the ground before Lockjaw, but the latter had eyes only for the softness of the buckskin and the gaudiness of the beads. He slipped into the garment and swelled up proudly, looking down at the star which now graced his chest. "Reckon I'll keep that, too," he observed. "I allus did hanker to find a star toter what was somethin' like a *man*. I reckon this here's the only chanct I'll ever have to see my dreams come true."

He patted the vest with satisfaction, felt something in the inner pocket and took it out, while the sheriff glared furiously. *"Hunh!"* Lockjaw grunted. "Legal papers and everything—what's in this here packet? Wouldn't be money now, would it?"

"Whatever it is, it's goin' to be bad luck to you!" the sheriff snarled. Lance, watching the change in his eyes, immediately became convinced that the packet did contain money. But Lockjaw had asked the question merely to irritate the lawman, and instead of opening the packet, he opened the legal paper.

"The last will and testament," he read aloud, "of Frederick Holcomb."

"What?" the question broke from the girl, impulsively. "Why, that's Uncle's will—his!" She gestured toward the dead body of the elderly man.

Doc Grimson's eyes narrowed. "Then what were you doing with it?" he shot at the sheriff suddenly.

The girl, too, was looking at the lawman in a curious, puzzled way.

"I had it because he give it to me, to be filed," the sheriff flared. "That's what I'm doin' with it. And if you know what's good for you, you'll give it back."

"How come you didn't ask for it before?" Lance asked softly. "You knew it couldn't be any use to us."

"I was hopin' that lunkhead wouldn't find it," the lawman snarled. "I know what's in it, and so do two witnesses, but there ain't no tellin' what use a gang of crooks like you would try to make of it."

"And just what is in it?"

"He leaves everything he's got to his niece, Elizabeth Holcomb—that's what's in it!" the sheriff answered, his eyes glacial. He turned to the girl and said, "He give it to me last night, Beth. Losin' it wouldn't have done no harm. There's me and the witnesses to say it's yours—and there ain't nobody to dispute it, I reckon. Since you come from the East, it's been pretty generally knowed that he'd leave the ranch to you."

Beth Holcomb's expression changed, softened. "I—I understand, Cousin Blaze," she said. "It's all right."

" 'Cousin Blaze!' " Doc rapped out. "Do you mean to say that you're this girl's cousin? How's it happen you're not included in the will?"

"That's none of your business!" the sheriff told him hotly.

"No? But you *were* included in a former will, weren't you?" Doc asked shrewdly.

A tide of color swept up over the lawman's granite features. For the first time he looked disconcerted. Then he recovered himself and answered savagely. "That's none of your business, either. What are you tryin' to insinuate, you skunk?"

Lance Clayton's eyes had taken on the tint and temperature of river ice. His big shoulders were hunched a little as he leaned toward the sheriff and asked, "Just what were you doin', amblin' around here this morning? You and your four partners?"

THE LAWMAN hesitated an almost imperciptible instant, then said, "I was lookin' for you, since you want to know. Had word that you were comin' this way. Are you tryin' to make out that I'd murder my own uncle? You fool, I've got four witnesses to every move I've made this mornin'. Don't think you can lay any of your own dirty murders on me."

"Don't worry about that, Cousin Blaze," the girl flashed indignantly. "It would take more than the insinuations of beasts like these to make anybody believe such a thing of you!"

"Who were these two witnesses to the will?" Doc asked suddenly.

"Who do you think you're cross-examining?" the sheriff snarled at him. Then he turned to Beth Holcomb. "You'd just as well know, Beth," he said significantly, "because I may have to get myself killed wringin' the neck of one of these skunks here. The witnesses was Saint McGee and…" he halted, a startled expression crossing his face. "Holy Moses!" he muttered, as though to himself, "I forgot!"

When he went on again his face was grave. "The other," he told the girl, "was Seth Hornsby." His gesture indicated the dead body which lay next to the stockman's.

"Of course," the girl said softly, "it would be Seth. Seth had been his foreman for years." But Lance thought that her expression, as she spoke, was a little queer.

"One of the witnesses died then!" Lance pointed out, grimly. "And the other… who is he?"

"A friend of mine," the girl answered coldly. "And now I'll have that will, please!"

Lockjaw still held the paper. He made no motion to hand it to the girl, but instead looked at Charlie Parr, who looked at Doc.

"I think," Doc said thoughtfully, "that we'll just hold that paper awhile—as exhibit A." He turned to the girl. "You can feel perfectly easy about it, ma'am," he said. "It will be safe with us."

The girl flared up indignantly. "You're quick to accuse Sheriff McArthur," she said. "But you prove that you're dishonest in the next breath."

Before Doc could reply to that, Charlie Parr snapped, "Here they come! Get movin'!"

The figure of a horseman had appeared on the ridge, silhouetted against the sky. Behind him, another appeared.

"Help, Jud! Help!" the girl screamed suddenly.

The figures stood immobile for a split second, then one slid from the saddle with a rifle in his hand and dropped to the ground, while the other disappeared behind the ridge. The group below could hear this second man shouting, "Trouble here, boys! Come a-foggin'!"

"Horses!" snapped Doc Grimson. "Lead the way, Charlie." In the saddle he addressed Blaze McArthur, "In case any of you want to lean on lead goin' past, just try something before we've got a good start."

An instant later, led by Charlie Parr, the five plunged downhill into the brushy woods on the right of the trail. As they did so, there was the crack of the Winchester from the crest of the ridge. Following on the report, a compact dozen riders broke the skyline and whirled shouting down the slope.

The sheriff's posse leaped for their guns, which had been thrown into the bushes. The men were already in the saddle when the other group came up to them.

"The Five Mavericks!" Blaze McArthur yelled by way of explanation, "They've killed Holcomb and Seth Hornsby!"

There was a chorus of infuriated yells and curses from the new group, and all together the riders went crashing into the woods in reckless pursuit.

Lance Clayton bent low in the saddle to escape the overhanging branches, risked a glance over his shoulder. He knew that the affair was going to be touch and go. The sounds told him that the pursuers would have been within shooting range had it not been for the trees and thick growth. And even as he looked, he caught glimpses through the branches of plunging horses and men behind him.

Lockjaw, lagging unaccountably behind, apparently saw them well enough to think he could do some damage. He turned deliberately in the saddle, leveled his six-gun and let fly.

"Come on, Lockjaw," Lance yelled. "Never mind shooting—you can't stop 'em here."

Lockjaw appeared not to hear. His horse was slackening speed more and more, and he himself continued his slow deliberate triggering. Lance pulled his mount in. With a hornet's nest of nearly a score of reckless riders pounding along their back trail thirsting for their blood, spurred on by the ruthless killings attributed to the Mavericks, Lockjaw's actions amounted to suicide. But Lance couldn't leave him to face the attack alone. Even as he wheeled his horse to go back and pound some sense into Lockjaw's thick, loyal skull, Lockjaw's horse staggered to a halt, stood trembling a moment and then went down.

LANCE DROVE back toward him, conscious at the same time that Charlie Parr had seen what had happened and was riding at his side. Together they yelled to Lockjaw that they were coming, but Lockjaw merely waved his hand and plunged off to one side in the bushes on foot. When the two arrived at the side of his fallen horse, he had disappeared entirely.

"No use goin' after him," Charlie said curtly. "He'll take care of himself. Let's try to hold 'em off long enough to give him a good start."

Lance nodded briefly as his hands flashed to his Colts. The first pursuers were now not more than a hundred yards away, visible at intervals as their mounts slid and twisted downhill through the trees.

Lance's right gun, then his left, roared and bucked. Beside him, Charlie Parr's worn, deadly "hawglegs" bellowed a staccato thunder in his ears, spaced and regular as the beat of a giant geyser of death.

Ahead of them a horse went to his knees, somersaulted, hurling his rider with jarring force against the trunk of a tree. Another reeled in his saddle, swung outward and down. A third clutched his hip with an agonized gesture and fought to haul his excited pony in.

Two men near him pulled up at the same time and slid from their saddles, taking cover behind tree trunks. Those were angry men, but even anger is likely to take counsel with caution when it is confronted by such deadly shooting.

Someone yelled, "They're makin' a stand. We've got 'em!" Blaze McArthur's voice crackled. "Spread out and circle 'em!" There was the sound of horses moving wide in obedience to the order.

Doc and Flint rode up, brought back by the sound of the firing.

"Lockjaw's bronc is down—he went off on foot," Charlie explained briefly as his practiced fingers flicked cartridges into the hot cylinders of his guns. "Hope the lunkhead don't get caught in the circle. We better fog. What's below?"

"River," Flint told him. "Looks bad."

"Can the broncs swim it?"

"Might," Doc answered laconically.

"Let's go, then. Once we git on the other side, won't nobody else be able to cross it."

A puncher in front, deceived by the silence, yelled, "They're gettin' away. Come a-shootin'!" In his excitement, he threw caution to the winds and jumped to his feet. Doc Grimson's guns spoke twice, whistling lead around his ears. The man dropped back with a startled expression and began to shoot.

Charlie Parr shook his head as lead cut the leaves which concealed them. "You'd ought to have winged him, Doc," he observed. "Them fellers ain't playin' marbles for fun."

"He's one of Miss Holcomb's men," Doc said. "No use messing them up more than necessary. Under the cut here, there's a moss path. Let's take it quiet. They won't know we've got away."

To the right of them, as they moved away, there was a sudden burst of firing, shouts, and then silence. "Lockjaw!" observed Charlie Parr grimly.

"You think they got him?" Flint asked. "Maybe we ought to ride that way."

"Naw!" Charlie told him contemptuously. "That dumb coot's a Injun in the woods. They won't never git a glimpse of him."

The moss path ended. "Let's go!" Doc snapped. Their spurred mounts were off in a break-neck run. Yells behind them told them that the others had heard the sounds of their going, but before the pursuers got back into their saddles the four had increased their lead by precious yards.

A BREATHLESS course through tangled brush and thinning trees brought them out suddenly on the all-but-flooded banks of a foaming, rushing stream. At sight of it, Charlie Parr's eyes widened and his face was doubtful. Lance Clayton whistled softly.

There was no sign of any ford. The brown, swirling waters swept past, deep, swift, forbidding. For two hundred yards the flood fled smoothly between banks eighty yards apart, but then it narrowed, swiftening, between the walls of a canyon, and the rocks began—jagged, upthrust rocks about which the brown water boiled up in dirty foam. And between them deep waves, crested and back-curling, marked underwater rocks were even more treacherous and deadly. Beyond these rapids, the canyon narrowed still further and the river became a hissing, bubbling torrent of foam before it plunged thunderously over falls.

There would be no chance for any living thing which was caught in that roaring, spume-flung hell. A man, a horse, would be dead, battered into something scarcely recognizable, even before he was swept over the falls. The horses would have to swim the eighty yards to the opposite bank before the current swept them down into the boiling rapids. It would be touch and go.

Behind them their escape was cut off. No doubt it was cut off on all sides now—unless they wanted to try to shoot their way through nearly overwhelming odds. They might do it, but almost certainly some of them would be left there, dead, before they came through.

For the space of two heartbeats they hesitated there. Then Doc Grimson, his features impassive, shoved his horse into the water. Flint Maddox, grim-faced, followed him. The animals were scarcely shoulder deep before the savage force of the current struck them, sweeping them from their feet, and sent them rolling helplessly downstream. Then the frantic strokes of their legs steadied them, sent them out toward the farther bank.

Charlie Parr still held back. For a second it looked as though his iron nerve might fail him at last. The color had drained from the brown leather of his features, and his eyes were foreboding with the sudden premonition of death.

Lance Clayton, seeing the fear that gripped the older man, sat his saddle motionless. If Charlie chose to face the guns instead of the river, he, Lance, would face them with him. He knew suddenly that Charlie would rather die twenty times over of gun-fire than face the terror of the gasping, choking death which lived in those foaming waters.

And then Charlie Parr's shoulders straightened. He looked around at Lance; the mouth beneath the flowing white mustache stretched in an engaging grin; the ageless blue eyes twinkled with sudden humor.

"I allus did hate water," he said—"inside or out!" He put decisive spurs to his horse. "Don't neither of us like it, bronc," he said dryly, "but git in, anyway!"

Lance Clayton's throat tightened and he set his teeth hard to keep back the sudden moisture which stung his eyes. That was the way the kind of man Charlie Parr was showed yellow! Yellow? Hell, Charlie didn't know what the term meant. He knew fear, though—and then, with his twinkling grin, he went right ahead to meet it!

A moment later Lance's own mount was struggling in the current. Lance slipped easily from the saddle and swam alongside, his left arm moving in powerful strokes that lightened the weight on the right on the saddle horn.

CHAPTER 3
TWO-WAY DEATH!

I T WAS soon apparent that his horse was a better swimmer than Charlie's, just as Lance was a better swimmer than its leather-faced rider. He watched with apprehension as the gap between himself and the older man widened. There was nothing he could do to stop that, nothing but swim and hope that the other would come through all right. Gradually, however, he saw that Charlie, though he would land farther downstream, would easily make the opposite shore before the current swept him into the rapids.

Doc and Flint had almost reached the other bank, and Lance himself was getting well in when a burst of firing blasted from the woods behind him. The pursuers had come into sight of their quarry. Bullets zipped into the water on both sides of him, but the sound of the shots advised him without his looking around, that the lead came from six-guns instead of rifles. At that range, the Five Mavericks might escape unless the posse-men were experts with a Colt.

He had scarcely thought that when there came the sharp, unmistakable crack of a carbine and a rifle bullet zipped by his head, to cut the water just in front of him. That was too close for comfort. Another rifle spoke, then another.

Doc, then Flint, drew out on the bank and whirled, drawing

Winchesters from their saddle scabbards. Lance quit swimming, grabbed the pommel with his left hand and reached for a Colt with his right. If he could help to draw the fire from Charlie....

As he turned to aim, he saw why the rifle fire had so far been ineffective. The group which had emerged from the woods behind had been too impatient to dismount and they were firing from the backs of broncos, half wild from the excitement of that chase downhill through the woods. But as Lance let fly his first shot, praying inwardly that the water had not ruined his ammunition, Sheriff Blaze McArthur slipped from the back of his rearing mount and knelt, steadying his rifle with an elbow

on his knee. Lance's gun had gone off on the first shot with the old, familiar bucking roar, but now as he tried to fling a hasty slug at the kneeling marksman, it missed fire.

He cursed, seeing McArthur's Winchester spurt smoke even before the report came to his ears. There was a cracking thud behind him, to the left, and Charlie Parr's horse went under with a gasping grunt, his rider with him.

For a wild instant, Lance considered trying to turn back, but it would have been mere useless suicide, as he realized even before the thought took form in his mind. Charlie was farther downstream than he was. There would be no chance of overtaking him. To attempt it would be merely to condemn himself and his struggling mount to the deadly menace of the rapids.

There was nothing to do but get to shore as fast as possible. Maybe by riding downstream….

He shoved his six-gun back into its holster and struck out again with the left arm, urging his horse to greater speed. Vaguely, he was conscious that Doc and Flint were firing from the opposite shore and that the shooting behind him had lessened. A glance over his shoulder showed him that Charlie had bobbed to the surface and was making feeble effort to swim toward the shore. But Charlie was no swimmer. It was as much as he could do to keep himself afloat. He would never make any progress against the savage force of that current. Lance groaned. If only he could give his own horse to Charlie, he himself could have made it unaided.

He felt his horse's feet strike land, pulled himself into the saddle as the animal struggled ashore. Doc was still there, under cover in the bushes, but Flint had disappeared. Lance guessed that he had ridden downstream. Without pause, he turned his horse and spurred him into a gallop through the brush which lined the shore.

As he did so, Lockjaw appeared on the opposite shore. Lance could see that he had seen the plight of Charlie Parr from the expression of agony and horror on his normally wooden features.

For an instant only, Lockjaw hesitated, then he shucked the sheriff's gaudy vest, his gunbelt and his boots in a series of movements which set a record in speed for Lockjaw. An instant later, Lance saw him in the water, swimming, not for the shore, but downstream in a hopeless attempt to intercept Charlie Parr.

Lance cursed, groaning. Charlie himself was already almost too far downstream for even a strong swimmer to have saved himself from the rapids. Lockjaw would miss him and be carried downstream himself.

And in fact, Lockjaw, shaping his course farther and farther downstream, misjudged his distance, and by cutting off at too sharp an angle, did miss him. But instead then of trying to save himself by swimming toward the bank, Lockjaw turned even more directly downstream, striving with his slow but immensely powerful strokes to overtake the bobbing white head in front of him. And Lance, watching as his horse raced along the bank, knew that Lockjaw would succeed—would overtake the man he had followed so many years with unquestioning dog-like loyalty, just as he entered the white water below, the slick. They would go into that raging destruction together. And Lance knew, too, that for once Lockjaw was not acting merely because he had room in his thick head for only one idea at a time. He had deliberately chosen death, rather than watch the man he loved go out without him.

"The danged fool," Lance half sobbed under his breath. "The danged, thickheaded fool!" But he knew in that final moment that he had seen clear into the soul of Lockjaw Johnson and that what lay there was greater than mere cleverness could ever be.

FLINT MADDOX, who had taken a route through the woods, appeared suddenly on the bank before him and pulled up, lariat in his hand. His anxious eye searched the stream and when it fell on Charlie Parr's bobbing head, his shoulders slumped. Seeing that, Lance knew that Flint had had the same slim hope that he had had—and that that hope was futile. Charlie Parr had, by a freak of the current, been carried too far toward midstream to be reached by a forty foot lass' rope.

For a second, Lance sat immobile at Flint's side, his mind racing frantically for some trick, some way to check the fatal progress of those two figures sweeping toward destruction. But he and Flint were almost at the beginning of the white water. In seconds now, Charlie Parr would be opposite them, past them—beyond any human help.

Suddenly Lance slipped from the saddle with a muffled exclamation, dropped his gunbelts and tore at his boots with frantic hands. He had seen one last chance. Out in the stream, some thirty or forty feet above the first of the white water, was flat rock, perhaps a yard square, about which the hastening current foamed, but whose surface was clear of the water. If he could reach that rock!

It was a desperate chance. It was doubtful whether even such a strong swimmer as he knew himself to be could cut out to that rock against the force of the racing brown waters. And even if he did manage that, could he get a grip and hold on? And if he managed to do that, would he be in time? The questions raced through his mind without checking the lightning swiftness of his movements, and before he had even got them well-formulated he had slipped the coil of his lariat about his neck and plunged headfirst into the stream.

He dived flat, shoving off with all the power of his legs, and came up in a powerful, racing stroke, arms flailing like pistons overhead, looking up only for instantaneous flashes to keep his direction true. The moment the current took him in, he knew his chances were small. The water was faster, much faster, here. Looking at it from the bank gave no conception of its resistless force. He shaped his course further upstream, fighting with all his strength and skill to get outward distance before the stream carried him below his objective, and, inevitably, into the rapids below.

One of his kaleidoscopic flashes showed him the two heads, closer together now but still upstream from himself. If he could make the rock, he might have a chance, just a chance to get a rope to them.

But it didn't look as though he were going to make the rock. He was going downstream with terrifying swiftness. With set teeth and straining muscles he forced more power, more speed out of himself, driving his arms deep and striving to quicken the beat of his legs. It was all over in a few blind, breathless seconds; seconds that seemed endless in their agony of suspense. A glance ahead showed him the rock almost within arm's reach but slipping past him upstream like a flash. A final frenzied effort, and his left hand clutched the upper edge, slipped on the smooth, worn surface, missed—and clutching, caught in the rough jut of a crevice!

His body, swept downstream, brought up with a jerk against the current which nearly loosened his grip. Frenziedly he clawed with his right hand for the flat, dry top, again found a grip—just in time, for his left hand was slipping. With a sudden, desperate heave, he drew himself up, got on top.

Charlie Parr's head, grim-faced, desperate, was sweeping by opposite him. Lance could see his mouth open, gasping for breath. His arms were clawing the water before him in feeble strokes that kept letting his head go under. Behind him, the great sweep of Lockjaw's arms were bringing him closer and closer. Another few strokes and he would be within reach of the older man.

There was no time for Lance to think or breathe. He would have just one chance, one throw, before the pair swept by him. Would the rope reach that far? Could he throw it, wet, with enough accuracy to snare that struggling, bobbing white head? The questions were in his mind almost without his being conscious of them, as his right arm swung, building his loop.

If only Charlie Parr would look! If he could catch at the loop, Lance's chances of missing would be lessened. "Charlie! Charlie!" he shouted. "Rope coming! Catch it!" But Charlie, at grips with death, did not hear.

With a half-uttered prayer, Lance threw. The narrow loop sailed clean, driving for its mark with the graceful, precise flight of a bird. It sailed true—and fell short by a foot!

CHARLIE PARR did not even see it. Half-strangled,

blinded, gasping, the slap of the rope on the surface meant nothing to him. He swept past it.

Not so Lockjaw!

His flailing right arm dove through the loop without interrupting the oar-like stroke which sent his outstretched left hand within reach of Charlie's head. Iron fingers twined themselves in the older man's hair, gripped hard. The rope tautened, snapped tight as the two bodies brought up short against the current. Lance, gripping tight with his free hand, was nearly wrenched from his perch on the rock.

Charlie and Lockjaw swept in an arc at the rope's end until they were directly downstream from Lance. Lance dragged himself to the upper edge of the rock and slipped his legs in the water until his knees had a sure grip, then, hand over hand, straining, he dragged the pair up to the rock. With Lockjaw's help he got Charlie up on the rock, where he sat gasping and choking.

Lance had been vaguely conscious of the faint sound of cheering and yells of approval. Now he looked to see half a dozen of the punchers and possemen who had been pursuing them grouped on the bank some distance upstream. The smooth wall of the canyon into which the stream poured as into a funnel extended farther on that side and had stopped the men some distance away, but they had seen what had happened clearly enough. Their cheering was the instinctive tribute of real men to a feat of bravery and skill.

Almost immediately the cheering died down and Sheriff

McArthur's voice came in a clear, far-carrying shout: "We've got you men! Stay where you are until we can help you off."

But Flint and Doc had had time by then to splice a couple of reatas together. Now Flint called out, "Rope coming, Lance— get it!"

The first throw missed. Blaze McArthur yelled, "Quit it—or we'll drill you!"

Flint gave no sign of having heard him. As calmly as though he were roping on his own range, he recovered the long lariat and built his loop again. McArthur dropped to his knee, training the rifle on him. At the same instant, Doc Grimson flung up his Winchester and fired, off-hand.

McArthur's rifle leapt from his hands and hit the ground several yards behind him. Doc Grimson had shot for the body and the slug had struck the rifle by accident, but Doc was a poker player and knew how to take advantage of his luck. "The next one will be for the man!" he yelled, nonchalantly.

Silence, which had somehow an air of bewilderment, greeted that. It was apparently a miraculous shot, and no one appeared to want to try conclusion with its author. Moreover, Lance guessed, those men who had cheered would have little heart for backing the sheriff's play under the circumstances. Later, when the three had gotten ashore again, all bets would be off, and the men who hunted them for the murder of their boss and foreman would be as ruthlessly bent on getting them as before.

Flint's second throw reached the rock. Lance caught it deftly and slipped the loop over Charlie Parr's head and under his armpits. Then he and Lockjaw took hold and all three slipped off the rock. But as they did so, Lance looked far upstream to see pursuing riders already swimming their mounts across. He remembered that they themselves had three horses among five of them and that they were in a strange country. The odds were still against them, backed by a hornet-mad law posse, plus a vengeance-hungry county!

CHAPTER 4
MAVERICK TRAIL

FLINT SET his heels in the soft dirt of the bank and drew the three Mavericks in hand over hand, while Doc stood with his rifle over his arm, watching for the first hostile move from the group on the other side.

But the watchers on the other bank evidently had changed their plans, for the moment the three stepped safely ashore, they jumped for their horses and rode at a gallop upstream. Evidently they intended to join the others who were crossing over. It would not be long before the pursuit was as hot as ever. And it came to Lance, with a shock of astonishment, that probably not five minutes in all had elapsed since the killing of Charlie Parr's horse! It seemed to him that the space had been long enough to include the events of a life-time, yet actually there had been only enough time for the bulk of the pursuing party, to reach the river's bank, to be driven to cover by Doc Grimson's fire, and to decide to ride upstream to a safer place to cross.

One of the horses' hoofs slipped on the rotted bark. Behind in the
woods, the sound of pursuing men and horses grew more plain.

Doc Grimson said curtly, "We'd better hit the breeze. Charlie,
you crawl up with me. Lance can take Lockjaw—that stallion
of his is stronger than Flint's horse."

Charlie Parr said awkwardly, "I'm kind of obliged to all you
boys—especially to Lance and Lockjaw."

Lockjaw looked sulky. Lance bristled. "What's the matter,

old timer—softenin' up on us? Maybe we could all join in a little hymn!"

Charlie waved a careless hand. "Oh, I know it ain't much of a life you saved," he remarked, grinning. "I wouldn't have said nothin' about it, only for wantin' to cover up that there rotten throw you made out there. If it hadn't been for Lockjaw bein' dumb enough to stick his hand through it, you'd have missed, complete."

He climbed nimbly behind Doc and they set off at a sharp trot. The others followed, Lance grinning broadly. Lockjaw said, after a moment, "He was wrong about that, though. Charlie, I stuck my arm through that loop *on purpose!*"

They angled to the left, away from the direction of the pursuit, until their course brought them to a deep, narrow ravine, the walls of which were too steep to offer any possibility of their getting down.

Charlie Parr swore. "That does it!" he exclaimed disgustedly. "Trapped, that's what we are—like a bunch of greenhorns!"

Lockjaw looked at him, surprised. "Shucks," he said with the apologetic air he had whenever he argued with Charlie. "I don't see that. There ain't no signs of 'em behind us. All we got to do is to follow along here until we find a way to cross."

"There ain't to be any signs of them behind us," Charlie snapped. "The pursuit's goin' to be from in front, this time!"

"You think they're ridin' to cut us off?" Flint asked.

"Certain," Charlie told him. "We're in an angle, with the river behind us and an uncrossable ravine on our left. Half of 'em will be closing in, slow, on our right flank, while the other half is ridin' hell-for-leather to git in front of us before we can get to a crossin'."

"If they're spread out thin that way, we can break right through," remarked Lockjaw complacently.

"With two horses double-loaded and wet ammunition," Doc

Grimson returned dryly. "Not to speak of the fact that they're three to our one."

"We got to find a way across this canyon," Charlie Parr said grimly. "Come on!"

Lance stared at him and whistled. "Be blamed if you didn't hang onto them old hawglegs of yours!" he marvelled, unbelieving.

Charlie looked back at him with a twinkle. "Thought there was somethin' weightin' me down," he said, "but I was too busy keepin' up to think what it was."

They rode on at a walk, listening. For a time there was silence. Their pursuers seemed to have vanished into thin air. Once Lance thought he heard far off hoof-beats and the crashing of underbrush ahead and to the right, but he could not be sure.

The forest through which they were making their way was of mixed growth in which pines predominated. Their own progress, therefore, was silent; the beat of the hoofs muffled by the carpet of pine needles.

Ahead of them a horse whinnied. It was answered by another to one side. To the right, still far off, something crashed in the bushes and hoofs clattered suddenly on rock. The cordon was closing in!

"Pull up, Doc," Charlie Parr said softly.

Lance believed that he meant to make a stand, but neither he nor Doc gave any orders. Doc looked at Charlie, waiting, as though he had caught some peculiar significance in his voice, but Charlie merely stared abstractedly at the trunk of a great tree which had fallen and lay across the canyon.

41

The opposite wall here was appreciably higher than the ground on which they, stood, so that the tree made a steep incline as its length soared out and up across the chasm. It was an old tree, rotted, the surface of the trunk slick with decay.

"Great Lord, Charlie!" Doc Grimson protested, as though the former had said something.

Lance stared and felt a shiver run down his backbone as the same idea began to come to him.

CHARLIE PARR pointed to where a spur of rock ran back through the woods, its near end within a couple of yards of the base of the fallen trunk.

"If we rode alongside the rocks, like we was anglin' off on them to cover our tracks, and then come back on 'em to the tree…" he said.

Doc Grimson shrugged. "I'm willing," he said, resignedly.

"You mean you're goin' to cross that tree," Flint Maddox asked incredulously. *"On horseback?"*

"I wouldn't try it on any broncs but these," Charlie argued, "but I think there'd be a good chance with them."

Flint, who was nearest the canyon edge, stared down into the depths, fifty or more feet below. Some of the color drained from his face. "I'm thinkin' that bath maybe made you a little wild, Charlie," he said, "but I'm willin'."

Lance thought, "Two of us could go on foot," but almost immediately it came to him that there wasn't much choice. A man would have to have sure feet and nerves to make that climb.

Somewhere ahead a horse stumbled, went crashing through the brush. Lance judged that the sound could not be more than two or three hundred yards away. There was no time now for further talk or thought. They moved off, Doc and Charlie in the lead, angling toward the spur of rock as though they were setting a course out to the right. Then they turned back on the rocks to the tree trunk.

Doc's horse put a tentative hoof on the trunk, tried to turn off to the right, then the left. It trembled, snorted once, and then mounted the tree trunk, moving along the thick bole with dainty, careful steps. Flint followed. Then Lance. Lockjaw slipped to the ground. "The two of us are too heavy," he whispered. Lance nodded. He was right, and besides, he would be safer so. No height, no matter how dizzy, would be apt to turn that stolid head of Lockjaw's!

The horse which carried Doc and Charlie was out over the chasm now, and already the trunk began to narrow. Before they reached the other side it would be no greater than the thickness of a small man's body. One of the horse's hoofs slipped on the rotted bark. He stood still, shaking. Doc Grimson spoke to him softly, gathered him, pressed gentle, firm spurs into the trembling flanks. The animal tossed his head and moved forward, slowly, carefully.

The trunk narrowed, its incline steeper. Lance no longer paid any attention to what was going on ahead of him. His own animal was in mid-chasm now. He devoted all his attention to sitting firm and even in the saddle, scarcely daring to breathe, as the stallion picked his sure-footed way. Behind him, in the woods, the sounds of the movement of men and horses grew more and more plain. He knew his own danger was double now. A shot from behind would do for him just as surely as a misstep by his horse.

Doc's and Charlie's horse suddenly came into view, going up the opposite slope. They had made it! His pulses pounded at the knowledge. Would Flint make it? Would he himself? He risked a glance down into the yawning depths of the gorge but wrenched his gaze away with an effort as he felt his head begin to turn. His throat was dry.

Flint's animal came to the opposite wall and, over-anxious, tried to increase his pace. He slipped, caught at the bank with his forelegs, fought his way, scrambling, upward.

Lance could hear voices in the woods behind him now. He wondered whether they would come in sight of himself and Lockjaw before they got off the log. Cautiously, he turned his head to see how the latter was coming along. What he saw made him forget the danger in a kind of irritated admiration. Lockjaw was standing over the middle of the chasm, facing the woods, with the Winchester he had borrowed from Flint slung carelessly over his arm. His pose was that of a hunter who stops to admire a pleasant view.

The stallion took the last few feet of the bole with the delicate sure-footedness of a mountain goat and Lance felt solid earth under him. He thought that nothing ever had felt so good to him.

He wanted to yell at Lockjaw, but instead pitched his voice low. "Lockjaw! Come *on!*" he murmured urgently.

Lockjaw turned, saw that Lance had gotten to the other side and began to walk toward him, with a rapid, lumbering step.

He looked awkward enough to fall off at every pace but apparently he had no fear of it. He looked entirely unconcerned.

They found the others watching them from the cover of some nearby brush. Lance saw Doc's Winchester over his arm and Charlie Parr's recently immersed Colts in his hands. Even with ammunition that missed fire at every other cartridge, marksmen on the other side would not have had a pleasant time trying to pick him and Lockjaw off!

A voice from below called excitedly, "Here's sign! They've come by here!"

THERE FOLLOWED a confusion of movement and talk as the others gathered, then Blaze McArthur's voice said, "You're right. They followed along to this ridge of rock and held to that to cover up their tracks."

"They couldn't have," somebody objected, "The ridge runs out to where we were closing in. They couldn't have got by without bein' noticed. Why, we'd a heard their horses on the rock even if we didn't see 'em."

"They had a good start," another voice put in. "They must have made better time than what we thought. They got through before we begun to close in."

"Or else the buzzards have got wings," McArthur agreed irritably.

"By gravy!" the other voice retorted, "it wouldn't surprise me none to find out they did have. If you ask me, I'd rather be chasing the devil himself than them Mavericks. Shoot, swim, ride—I never see nothin' like it!"

"An' stick together!" another put in. "You git your hands on one of 'em and you've got the other four a-buzzin' about your head, pronto. I ain't foolin', if it wasn't that they killed Fred Holcomb and Seth Hornsby, I'd be seekin' my fun elsewhere. I'd get me four-five mountain lions to tangle with if I felt like I was needin' some exercise!"

"Cut the gab," McArthur snapped irritably. "Let's follow along this rock spur until we cut their trail again. They must have left sign somewhere."

The group moved off. Lance could hear the sound of the horses' passage growing fainter and fainter in the distance.

Charlie Parr grinned. "Fooled 'em!" he commented, his eyes twinkling. "What's next on the program, Doc?"

"I say wait here awhile," Doc answered. "They may come back and figure it out that we crossed that tree. If they do, we want to know it. No use bargin' off, thinking that nobody's on our trail when somebody is. If they get on to us, they'll have to ride a long way around to get to us. We'd have time to get away, likely. And the way it is now, they'd be in our path if we wanted to get into town."

"I reckon you're right—but what I meant was, what's our next move after that? Looks to me like things is shapin' up kind of hard around here."

"The first thing to do is to find a way to get into town," Doc said grimly, "without endin' by decorating a cottonwood limb. We've got to look into the ways of this Sheriff McArthur. His having that will…."

Lockjaw clapped his hand to his head in a strangled snort

of horror. "Say!" he exclaimed. "I lost that vest—it had the papers in it!"

The others looked at him in mild surprise. They had all been aware from the beginning that Lockjaw had had to get rid of the vest and the papers. It was hard luck, but there hadn't been any way out of it.

"Don't worry about that, Lockjaw," Doc soothed him, "the girl...."

"The girl!" Lockjaw burst out excitedly. "The girl got it. I seen her when we was a-settin' on that rock. I seen her get off her horse just about the place I came out. She come up with somethin' in her hand."

"Calm down—calm down, amigo!" Charlie Parr advised him. "You ain't shore it was that she was pickin' up. She might be collectin' arrowheads—or discyarded airtights. Like enough, if we ever git back there, we'll find your things just where you dropped 'em."

Lockjaw merely muttered to himself. His mind was taken up with the conviction that the girl had gotten the vest and that it was, somehow, his fault. He had let the bunch down again! While that idea lodged in his mind, he would shed words of comfort as a slicker sheds water. Lance guessed that they would have little but gloom from Lockjaw until something happened which would be violent enough to dislodge his conviction of guilt.

The others, accustomed to the force with which simple and usually unimportant ideas took possession of Lockjaw's mind, disregarded him also.

Flint went off to picket the horses and stand guard over them. Charlie set about the preparation of some cold food. Lance went for water. Doc busied himself with cleaning guns and overhauling equipment.

When they assembled again to eat, Charlie Parr asked casually, "Where's Lockjaw?" Nobody knew, and a short search revealed no sign of him.

"Now where do you suppose that galoot would have wandered to?" Charlie wondered irritably.

Lance looked at Doc, in whose luminous gray eyes the cold devils of humor were dancing, and realized that they both had the same idea. "Shall I look?" he asked.

Doc grinned. "Might as well be sure," he assented.

Lance went up to the rise toward the canyon edge and, after a cautious glance at the other side, began to examine the ground. The first glance showed him what he sought—the marks of Lockjaw's stockinged feet, going back toward the log! HE RETURNED to the others and nodded at Doc. "He went back, all right," he confirmed.

Charlie Parr swore violently. "Across that log?" he asked, knowing the answer in advance.

"Without boots," said Lance drily.

"By gosh!" Flint exclaimed, "The crazy coot's gone back after that vest—I'll bet my bottom chip on it!"

Charlie Parr groaned. "That jarhead would go and mess things up! Now we'll have to go and look for him."

Doc Grimson shook with sudden laughter. "Miss Holcomb's goin' to be plumb surprised to see him," he chuckled.

Flint looked at him in surprise. "You think she really got the vest?" he asked.

"I haven't the least idea," Doc confessed. "But Lockjaw thinks she did—that's enough."

He got to his feet. "We can't get down that tree trunk again, so we've got a long way around to go. We'd better get movin'."

Working silently and efficiently they repacked their saddle bags and buckled on gunbelts. The sound of the posse returning on the bank below froze them into sudden immobility.

Out of a babble of talk McArthur's voice broke clear, "I'll tell you they must have," he snapped. "If they hadn't they'd have left some sign, somewhere."

Another voice said disgustedly, "Hell! There ain't a bronc alive that could walk that tree. Look at the slant of it and how it tapers off."

Then McAllister, triumphantly, "Look here! Look at the hoof marks at the base and the way the bark is broken off along the top of the trunk. Why there's even the clear print of a shoe!"

There was an instant of what seemed to be stunned silence, then the other voice said, stubbornly, "It's a bluff, I tell you. They could have walked a horse up on this thick part and then backed him down again. But there didn't no bronc go all the way over that tree."

"Maybe!" McArthur repeated, equally stubborn, "but I'm sure goin' to see."

A rider came pounding through the woods at a gallop, pulled up before the group. "Hey!" he yelled excitedly. "One of them fellers just pulled Hank off his horse—like to choked him to death!"

"See? What did I tell you?" the man who had been arguing with McAllister cried in triumph.

"Were the others with him?" McArthur snapped.

"No—only saw one."

"You let him get away?"

"I was too far off to stop him. I took a shot at him, but he was already most out of sight in the trees. I—I thought I better come tell you instead of trailin' him," he ended lamely.

The sheriff swore. "Look here, Bronson," his voice crackled on, "You're so sure they're on this side—you take half a dozen of your men and light out after that fellow that got Hank. The rest of us will ride around. I want to take a look at the other end of that tree. By God! I'll show these jaspers who they're playin' tricks on!"

Doc Grimson smiled faintly at Charlie Parr. "Nice to know their plans!" he murmured.

CHAPTER 5
LOCKJAW PLAYS HIS HAND

B ETH HOLCOMB had had the advantage of the non-combatant—she had seen a good deal, and she had had time to think about what she had seen. But her thoughts were not altogether pleasant.

She had not joined in the headlong pursuit of the Five Mavericks, knowing that, as a woman, she would only distract the attention of her own friends and thus complicate matters. But knowing the topography of the country she had sought high ground over the near wall of the canyon, from which point of vantage she could see what happened on the river. The incident of Charlie Parr's rescue had thus been clear to her in all its details. She watched it with mixed emotions—emotions which ended, however, in pure admiration.

When the two in the water had caught the rope, she rode down to the shore. Vaguely in her mind was the notion that her men must not be allowed to take advantage of the situation to fire at the men in the water. It was necessary for her to ride wide, however, to get down to the bank and her course brought her out at the point where Lockjaw had taken off the sheriff's beaded vest. By that time, her own purpose in coming down was no longer so clear. She had begun to tell herself that perhaps she should keep out of the affair, remembering that these men were the murderers of her uncle, and that they deserved little mercy from her.

The gaudy colors of the vest attracted her attention and she slipped down from her horse to pick it up. Without knowing just why she did so, she had decided to keep the will herself and stuffed the paper into the bosom of her blouse. The brown packet, like the vest, was obviously McArthur's private property and she intended to turn them both over to him at once. But by that time, the group on the shore had decided on their plan to corner the Five Mavericks in the angle of the river and the ravine, and they had gone sweeping past her at full gallop.

Again she sought her vantage point above the cliffs. The

countryside across the river was in plain view but so forested that she could see little beyond the tops of the trees, the deep cut of the ravine and a clearing or two.

Absently, she fingered the brown packet, wondering what it contained and remembering the stolid-faced outlaw's jeering suggestion that it might be money. The memory brought the whole scene back to her and set her thinking of the Maverick's attempt, as she still loyally phrased it, to cast suspicion on Blaze McArthur. But even as the idea formed in her mind she was conscious of a falsity in it when it was phrased that way. Those men had been so obviously sincere in their suspicions. She remembered the smoldering look in the eyes of the young blond man with the big shoulders and the slim hips, and the keen, luminous intelligence of the slender, dangerous-looking man who was called Doc Grimson.

She decided suddenly that they had not been acting—they really believed that Blaze McArthur might have murdered her uncle. And it came to her in a flash of illumination that if they believed McArthur had been the killer it was impossible that they themselves were guilty. Curiously, when that thought flashed on her, it brought an odd little feeling of relief. She realized, almost unbelievingly that she had already begun to like those men. She had been conscious that they had left a vivid impression on her—had struck her as being almost supermen.

She remembered how that blond Lance Clayton's arm had licked up like the tongue of a snake to land with crushing force on Blaze McArthur's jaw—remembered the astoundingly swift and unerring accuracy of Doc Grimson's rush; recalled with a half-smile of amused admiration the way Lockjaw Johnson had jumped feet first into the gunman's middle. And then that scene on the river! Who could have watched anything so magnificent as that without a tight throat and quickening pulses? Admiration, yes—awe, even. But liking? A few moments earlier she would have denied it, but now she had to acknowledge that chief among the qualities of these men who were called The Five Mavericks was that they were so likable! Strangely, they looked kind, as well as fearless and able. If she had met them without knowing who they were, she would have trusted them absolutely.

Of course, their suspicion of Blaze McArthur was absurd, but then they didn't know Blaze as she did. They couldn't be blamed for it. Blaze *might* have been her uncle's heir if she had not come West, even though Blaze's relationship to her uncle had not been as close as hers.

McArthur, in fact, was only her half-cousin. He was the son of a half-sister of Fred Holcomb's, who had run off with a gambler and adventurer, a man who had died outside the law. Blaze, at first, had followed in his father's footsteps. He had been known as a bad hombre—a gun-fighter and rambler who was looked on with suspicion by more than one sheriff. But Fred Holcomb had recognized some virtue in the boy, had brought him to the Bar BH, and eventually had gotten him elected sheriff. There had been a strong friendship between the older and the younger man, which the advent of Beth Holcomb had apparently done nothing to disturb. Beth was the daughter of Fred Holcomb's own brother, who, it had been thought, was pretty well fixed in the world. But his death had revealed that he was virtually bankrupt and Beth had come to live with her uncle. That had been two years ago.

ALMOST FROM the first there had been little question that Beth would supplant McArthur in her uncle's will. Fred Holcomb, in addition the affection with which he had showered her, had more than once indicated his belief that it would be unfair to give anything Beth needed to McArthur, who was a man, and could take care of himself in the world. And Blaze McArthur had shown in every way that he concurred heartily in that opinion. He had accepted Beth into his affections warmly as his cousin and friend, and Beth guessed that, with enough encouragement, he would have shown her an affection of a more serious sort.

It was as the thought of her cousin was in her mind that her eye caught a movement far up the twisting course of the canyon across the river. She thought casually that it looked like a big animal of some kind crawling across…. Suddenly, she leaned forward, straining her eyes. It wasn't possible! Hurriedly, she reached for the field glasses she carried in her saddle bags. As she did so, the brown parcel slipped from her fingers and fell to the ground. For the moment, she paid no attention to it. Her gaze was intent on what the glasses showed—the figures of two men, on a horse, crossing the old dead sycamore which lay across the canyon.

She knew the spot well, for the big fallen tree was a sort of landmark in the vicinity, and she could scarcely believe her eyes when she saw the Mavericks crossing it. Breathless, she watched as horse after horse came into view, made the perilous crossing and disappeared on the other side. After them, a man on foot, whom she recognized as Lockjaw Johnson, strolled by, like a figure on a Sunday promenade. When he had passed also, she sat back in the saddle with a sensation of weakness. It came to her suddenly that, no matter what she felt or did not feel, it would have no effect on those five men. They seemed capable of anything.

Then she remembered that she had dropped the packet and got down to get it. It was unsealed and the fall had thrown its contents half out of the envelope. For a second she stared with her mouth open and her heart stopped. What lay under her eyes was, in fact, money—greenbacks, the top one of which was a hundred dollar note. But it was not that which held her paralyzed while her brain whirled. Around the top sheaf of notes was a brown paper band, and on it was written the figures "$5,000." And the writing was in her uncle's hand!

Numb, she stooped and picked up the packet. There were two sheafs, exactly similar. Ten thousand dollars! For what could her uncle have given Blaze McArthur ten thousand dollars the night before he died?

Black suspicion invaded her mind. She knew something of the dead Holcomb's affairs, for she had acted as his secretary during the last year. She herself had helped him count the money which was in this packet, had watched him make the notation on the band before he pat it in his safe, where, habitually he kept large sums, divided into sheafs and labelled in that way. There could be no mistake about it. This money had come from her uncle's safe. And she could think of no possible business between him and his half-nephew which could have caused the transfer of such a sum to McArthur.

Then she remembered suddenly that that morning Fred Holcomb had been on his way to buy a herd of Herefords on which he counted to improve his stock. She did not know what the price of the herd was to be, but it must have been large. Would it be $10,000?

Of a sudden, she dropped her head in her hands with a groan. She had not realized how deep her affection for Blaze McArthur had been until this hideous possibility had come into her mind.

Miserably, she turned her horse and rode back toward the ranch. She tried to tell herself that her find was no real proof. Blaze might have some perfectly convincing explanation of his possession of the money. But in her heart she couldn't believe it. Why had he said nothing about the will being in his vest pocket when the outlaw had taken it? Why had he not mentioned the money during all that discussion of the will? Why should her uncle, have given him $10,000 just on that night? She remembered his past, remembered that he was known, despite his kindness to her, as a hard man. And she also remembered that her coming had cheated him out of a large inheritance. Was there another, prior will, through which he would have benefitted in case this present will had never been found?

Seth Hornsby had died—the only witness remaining would

be Saint McGee. Why had he not been killed, too? Had he any part in this? Her mind recoiled from the idea. She shook her head, her brain whirling. It was all impossible! Yet….

She turned her pony into the corral. The ranch seemed deserted, except for the cook. Tiredly, she went with dragging steps into the house, where she dropped into a chair in the big living room. For a long time, she sat there, with the will and the packet of money in her lap, staring at them fixedly as though they somehow could tell her what to do. Now she got up and went to the safe to put them both away.

She had just gotten the safe open when a step in the hallway caused her to look up, startled. Lockjaw Johnson stood in the doorway. He had his hat in his hand and his long, horse-like features wore an expression of embarrassment and determination.

"Excuse me, ma'am," he said, simply, "but I've come for that there vest and them papers."

THE GIRL stared at him for a moment, speechless. Then she said indignantly, "You really talk as though they were yours. They belong to myself and Sheriff McArthur, you know."

"No ma'am," stated Lockjaw doggedly. "We took 'em. They're our'n."

The girl stared at him; wordless, sheer astonishment beginning to replace the indignation in her expression.

"I'm shore mighty sorry to bother you, ma'am," Lockjaw apologized again but with undiminished determination. "You see the boys give me them papers to hold—leastways they didn't take 'em off me. The boys land of trusted me with 'em, so to

57

speak. An' dang if I didn't go an' lose my head and throw 'em away. I shore wish that there star-toter had've found 'em. I could of shot 'em loose from him. But you just give 'em to me, ma'am, an' that'll save trouble all around."

By this time, pure amusement had begun to replace the astonishment in the girl's eyes, just as the astonishment had driven out the anger. She remembered that this was the man whom she had seen swim down to certain death rather than abandon a partner. He had been forced to lose the papers because he had chosen to exhibit a brand of courage which was very nearly beyond belief. But her quick feminine intuition made her understand that Lockjaw was entirely incapable of thinking of himself as a hero. He was so little capable of it that he could remember only what he considered his fault in losing the things which had been entrusted to him!

She felt like bursting out into laughter; but she felt a little like crying, too. There was something pathetic as well as comic in the simplicity of this big, awkward, horse-faced, embarrassed, determined-looking man—in his simplicity and his lack of self-consciousness and his endless faithfulness. Any fear that she might have had of him vanished completely.

"Why—why, Lockjaw!" she said, simulating horror but scarcely able to keep the amusement out of her voice. "You wouldn't put your hands on a woman! What would the boys think of you if you did that?"

Lockjaw looked disconcerted. He didn't answer for a moment. Instead he stood staring at her, with his eyes troubled and his brow contorted by thought.

"I—I wouldn't go for to hurt you, ma'am," he stammered after a little. "You see, I—I just got to have them papers."

The girl put the will and the packet into the bosom of her blouse. "You see, you'd have to take them by force; Lockjaw. Why, suppose I had to tell Doc Grimson that you had done that—what would he say?"

Lockjaw's brow knotted still further. "I don't rightly know," he got out painfully. "I ain't never heard Doc say nothin' about that. But Charlie—he wouldn't like it, I reckon." His face cleared suddenly. "Why, shore!" he exclaimed, with an expression of relief. "I remember Charlie had an argyment with some of the boys because—why say!" his voice took on a tone of wonder. "It was just like this: some lady stood right in front of the safe and Charlie wouldn't let 'em touch her." His face flushed. "Yes, ma'am—you're shore right about that. I'm mighty glad you said what you did. Charlie would have give me hell—excuse me, ma'am, but that's what he'd of done—he'd of give me plumb hell for it."

Beth watched him in silence as he stood, apparently lost in self-congratulation at having escaped making so heinous a mistake. After a moment, however, his face fell. "But say!" he exclaimed, crestfallen, "that way, I won't git the papers back at all!"

The girl choked a little with laughter, but her eyes were soft. She felt as though she were denying a child something that would have made him happy. She sought for something to say that would comfort him and she hit at once on the one thing that might have done so.

"Did you and Charlie get what you came after that time when he wouldn't let the boys touch the lady?" she asked.

"Huh?" Lockjaw asked.

"What were you all doing that time when the lady stood in front of the safe?"

"Why, we was robbin' the bank."

"Did you get the money?"

"Why, no, ma'am. She wouldn't let us. I mean Charlie wouldn't let us. You see she was kind of standing with her arms spread out...."

"Then you went away without the money?"

"Yes'm. You see—"

"Well, it's the same thing now, isn't it? You're going away without the papers. Charlie's sure to say you did just right."

Lockjaw looked at her, dazed. Then his face beamed. "You shore do think things out fast, ma'am," he said, admiringly. He slapped his thigh suddenly.

"That's it! Shore as shooting, he's goin' to say I done right!"

There was a thud of hoofs out in the ranch yard. Beth stepped toward the window to see a tall, well-made man dressed in black dismount before the hitchrack.

"Well, ma'am," said Lockjaw, scraping his foot awkwardly and bobbing his head in what he evidently supposed was a gesture of politeness. "I reckon I better be hittin' the breeze. I left the boys back there an' they'll begin wonderin' where I been. I'm sorry I bothered you, ma'am...."

BETH WAS thinking rapidly. The rider out there by the hitchrack was Saint McGee. He was certain to have the description of the Five Mavericks—he might even have seen them somewhere. If he recognized Lockjaw…. She realized suddenly that she could not bear to have anything happen to Lockjaw Johnson.

"Wait a minute," she said swiftly. "Somebody's just ridden up. You'll have to hide."

Lockjaw looked alert. "How many of them are there?" he asked.

"There's only one. It's Saint McGee. He won't stay long."

Lockjaw looked surprised. "If there's only one," he asked, "what do I have to hide for?"

"It's Saint McGee," she told him hurriedly. "He might recognize you. Don't you know that there are thousands of dollars reward on every one of you?"

The slight tension went out of Lockjaw's features, "Is that all?" he asked. "Don't worry none about that, ma'am. Lots of other fellers have got themselves all het up about the reward money folks is always stickin' up for us. It don't do nothin' for 'em but start their health to gittin' bad."

"You don't know what you're saying!" the girl exclaimed in a low voice. "Saint McGee is a dangerous man. He's said to be one of the fastest men with gun…."

Lockjaw waved a large, ham-like, tolerant hand. "Shucks, ma'am," he said, grinning. "Don't you worry—we have us a few like that every mo'nin' for breakfast."

The rider in question had finished tying up his horse and was regarding the house with a questioning air. After a moment he began to walk toward the veranda.

Beth began to feel desperate. She realized that in calling Saint McGee dangerous, she had said the wrong thing. Woman-like, she changed her tactics with bewildering swiftness.

She went up to Lockjaw and smiled at him ravishingly: "Think how terrible it would be for me if there was any fighting," she said. "Won't you go into the next room—because I ask you to?"

Lockjaw flashed. "I won't start nothin', ma'am, if he don't," he said uncomfortably. "I don't like to be runnin' away from just one feller."

Beth put her hands on his shoulders and looked at him meltingly. "It might look so bad for me—if you were found here," she said softly. "You'll hide, won't you—on my account—Lockjaw?"

Lockjaw stared dazedly down into her eyes, drew in a long breath filled with the faint, intoxicating perfume of her hair, and rocked slightly on his heels like a man who has been punched hard in the jaw.

"Yes, ma'am," he stammered. "Shore, ma'am. I'll do anything…."

The girl put her finger swiftly to her lips in sign of silence as Saint McGee knocked sharply on the jamb of the open front door. She took the unresisting Lockjaw by the arm and led him to the door of a small room which opened off the living room and shoved him into it. "Stay there until I tell you to come out," she whispered, and shut the door quickly.

CHAPTER 6
THE SAINT'S GUN-GAME

SAINT McGEE, who had walked in following his knock, calling out cheerfully to know if anyone was at home, found her with her eyes dancing and her mouth quivering with the laughter she fought to suppress.

"You look mighty cheerful," he commented, glancing quickly around the room. "What's been tickling you?"

There was a faint overtone of surprise in his tone and Beth was suddenly recalled to a consciousness of the tragedy of her uncle's death. She wondered if the man before her had heard of it, and flushed with shame at the realization that it had been driven entirely out of her head.

She said simply, "How do you do, Mr. McGee?" She felt sobered, not only at the memory of her uncle but also by the presence of the man before her. She did not like Saint McGee very well, although she felt his fascination. Perhaps it was just those two facts taken together which made her always so reluctant to receive him. Something about the man frightened her. "He makes me feel a little like a sparrow looking at a diamondback," she had once told her uncle. She remembered that now, for no especial reason, and remembered, too, how Fred Holcomb had laughed in his big easy-going way. "I reckon it's not that bad," he had said, "although I reckon Saint can be about as dangerous as a rattler when he wants to be."

Just what her uncle's real attitude toward McGee had been she had never really discovered. Fred Holcomb was a man who, despite his easy-going heartiness, appraised men shrewdly and exercised an extraordinary discretion in airing his opinions on them. She had an idea that his feelings toward McGee had been mixed, that he had respected him as a successful man, eminently capable of holding his own in a hard country, but that he did not wholly like or trust him. She had thought that she had seen a certain concern in her uncle's manner when McGee's visits to the ranch-house had become increasingly frequent, but he had never by word or action indicated that the visitor was not welcome.

There was, indeed, no reason to do so. Saint McGee had been and still was a gambler, but he had the advantage of being a successful one against whom there had never been any charge of crookedness. Whether that latter fact was due to the reputation he had of being deadly with a gun or not, Beth had no way of knowing.

He owned and operated the largest saloon and gambling palace in Sageville. He was reputed to be making a lot of money and he was beginning to be a force in county life and politics. From Beth's Eastern point of view, the owner of a gambling house was not very high up in the social world but that was not so in the West, and, perforce, she had begun to adopt the simpler, Western way of looking at such things.

McGee, himself, was a more than usually personable figure. Tall, well-built, he kept himself immaculately groomed and his manners had an ease and polish which set him definitely apart from the ordinary citizen of that section. His dark, good-looking face was made extraordinary only by the eyes. They were a curious, bright, pale blue, widely opened and set wide apart, one of them a little higher than the other. They stared at you without much expression, even when his mobile, smiling features were most expressive. They seemed to lead a bright, emotionless life of their own, those pale, flaring eyes, apart from the rest of the man who was Saint McGee. It increased their fascination for Beth, because she could not read what was behind them. Courage was in them—that she felt sure. An insane sort of courage, even. And when Beth had first thought of that word "insane" it had made her uncomfortable, as if she had detected something a little mad in the opened wideness of Saint's eyes. Which was absurd, she told herself, because every move and words of the man showed him shrewder and more levelheaded than most.

Just now there was the barest glint of suspicion in his eyes as he completed his survey of the room. "Thought I heard you talkin' to someone," he remarked casually.

"It was just the cook," Beth told him calmly, "he's gone now. Will you sit down?"

"I wanted to talk to your uncle a minute, if I could."

Beth thought, "So he hasn't heard."

McGee, as he spoke, had taken a slip of paper out of his pocket. Now he continued without pause. "It's just a little matter of business between us," he smiled, motioning with the paper, "Won't take long. After that…."

Beth said gravely, "You'll have to take up your business with me, Mr. McGee—my uncle is dead."

The gambler looked shocked. "You don't tell me! Why—why I saw him only last night! What happened?"

Briefly, a little hesitantly, Beth told him what had happened that morning. She found herself somehow reluctant to involve the Five Mavericks in the story, but she told herself that McGee would learn the facts from somebody else very shortly. There was no use in trying to conceal anything. Of the contents of Blaze McArthur's pocket, however, and the suspicion they had aroused in her she said nothing.

Saint McGee listened to her account with his face growing more and more grim. "Those fellows have got to be run to earth," he exclaimed energetically when she had finished, "if it takes every man and every cent this county can put its hands on!"

The girl said, "You mean the men who murdered my uncle." Her tone had an enigmatic significance which the gambler either did not hear or chose to ignore.

"Why, yes," he said, still in his positive and grim manner. "I mean the Five Mavericks. They've committed enough crimes around here—and they've ended by murdering one of the finest men who ever lived in this county. It's time for them to die."

"I don't believe the Five Mavericks are guilty," the girl said, her voice defiant.

"Not guilty? How can you think that?"

"I've seen and talked to them. I believe somebody is impersonating them."

Saint McGee glanced at her sharply a surprised moment, then he said gravely. "I'm afraid you'd have a hard time convincing anybody of that. The evidence against them is too plain."

Beth Holcomb looked stubborn. "It seems plain," she said, "but it could be somebody else, and I believe it is."

McGEE LOOKED thoughtful. Presently he said gently, "If I were you, Beth, I wouldn't say that around much. There are people who would think it didn't sound well coming from you."

"What do you mean?"

"Only that—well, you benefit by your uncle's death. You mustn't give anybody a chance to say that you're trying to protect the men who killed him!"

The girl stared at him, speechless and outraged. Then she flared, "Are you daring to suggest that I had anything to do with…. Oh! how abominable!"

McGee raised a deprecatory hand. "My dear Beth!" he exclaimed. "*I* suggest anything? Nothing could have been farther from my mind. Don't you see that I want to be your friend? There are always people who are suspicious and mean-minded enough to think evil. I only want to avoid having you give those people a chance to set their tongues clacking. The evidence against these men is so strong…."

"I'm not afraid of what people will think, Mr. McGee." The gambler's ear did not escape the faint emphasis on the "mister."

He smiled affectionately. "Do you think I oughtn't to call you Beth? Won't you give me permission to? I have thought of you as Beth so long—and—well, if you knew how much affection there was behind that name when I say it, I think you couldn't be much offended at the liberty."

It was a graceful speech and it sounded sincere. Beth Holcomb felt a little ashamed and she softened at once.

"After all, why not?" she said forgivingly. "I'm sorry I got offended at what you said. I'm sure you want to be my friend."

"If only you knew how much!" he said, with a hint of ardor which sent the girl searching in her mind for an excuse to turn the conversation.

"What was the business you had with Uncle Fred?" she asked.

The gambler seemed suddenly reminded of the slip of paper which he still held in his hand. "Oh," he said, as though suddenly a little embarrassed. "That's nothing now. I reckon I'll just tear this little slip up and we can forget about it."

"Don't do that," the girl interposed. "Tell me what it is."

Saint McGee's slight air of confusion deepened. "Why it's nothing," he said hastily, "er—just a little IOU I held of his. I didn't aim to bother you with it, Beth."

"Oh, but I insist! Uncle's debts are mine now, you know. Let me have it please." Her manner had a pretty imperiousness in it to which the gambler yielded with apparent reluctance. He handed her the slip.

At the sight of it her face paled a little. "Twenty-two thousand and five hundred dollars!" she gasped, staring at the figures incredulously. "But—but—what in the world *for?*"

McGee said on a tone of sympathy, "It was just a gambling debt. I reckon you didn't know that your uncle used to plunge a little now and then. Of course, that's not very big money to him and I wouldn't have thought of bothering him with it, except that I've got a chance to buy in on a nice little spread and I was a little short of cash."

The girl stammered a little as she said, "I—I had no idea. Uncle had a pretty large sum of money on him this morning, which was taken—I'm not sure just how much cash...."

Saint McGee cut in, "Now, don't you worry about it. Come to think of it, I did hear your uncle saying that he had a good deal to meet right now—taxes and interest on his mortgages. I had completely forgotten about it. Don't you worry a bit. If somebody else held that they might put in a claim now for cash and start all your other creditors doing the same thing. It might be bad, if you've lost money already. But I told you before that I wanted to be your friend." He smiled reassuringly.

The girl continued to regard the slip of paper wonderingly and with a touch of horror in her eyes. It seemed inconceivable that her uncle had gambled to that extent. She didn't suppose he was above sitting in a little game from time to time, but to risk such a sum seemed out of character for him. There was something else, too, about this slip of paper which bothered her somehow, but whatever it was it had not succeeded in getting up into her consciousness.

She became aware that Saint McGee had come closer to her. His voice came to her ears in a tender murmer. "Beth, darling," he was saying, "why don't you let me take care of you? That little slip of paper would be nothing then. All in the family, that's all. Haven't you seen how much I cared for you?" He put his hands on her shoulders and began to draw her toward him.

His touch sent a sudden shiver down Beth's back, but it was

a shiver which was mostly fear. Something in her felt the attraction of the man, but something else, some deeper instinct, warned her against him. She found herself looking up into his eyes as though hypnotized, felt her body sway forward under his gentle propulsion. Then with a gasp of sheer panic she wrenched away. "Don't touch me! Don't touch me!" she cried, involuntarily.

SHE WOULD have felt ashamed of herself the next moment had not Saint McGee's expression hardened and sudden anger looked out of his eyes.

"You little—" he rapped out, but almost immediately caught himself up. "There's nothing to be afraid of, Beth," he said in another tone. "But don't you think you're being a little foolish? Are you in a position to be so independent?" He motioned, as he spoke, to the safe, the door of which still stood open behind her, and somehow the gesture included the IOU which the girl still held in her hand.

Beth realized suddenly that the curve of his well-shaped mouth was both sensual and cruel, and wondered dully why she had never seen it before. What was he doing—threatening her with this debt, after all he had just said about being her friend?

He reached out and took the paper from her hands. She was staring at it again and she gave it up unresistingly. But as she did so, the idea which had been struggling to the surface of her mind suddenly came through.

"Who wrote those figures?" she demanded suddenly.

"Your uncle wrote them, of course." The gambler's voice held a hint of ice in it.

The girl looked at him queerly, for the answer to her question had suddenly occurred to her. "I think he did," she said slowly. "I think he wrote part of them!" There was no mistaking the significance of her tone.

McGee's face flushed angrily. "What do you mean, you little fool?" he demanded. His staring, wide-open eyes were fixed upon hers and there was a sudden flare of cruel fury in them which reminded Beth of the impression she had once had of them. For one breathless second it was as though she had looked into the eyes of a maniac. Then the flare died out left them to their normal, pale brightness, but the light in them now was cold and still cruel. "Who do you think you're trying to play with?" he asked threateningly. "Hell, I can break you! I can break you in more ways than one. You think you can put up a fight against me? I'll show you!"

His voice had gotten thicker, more threatening; the sensual curl of his mouth heavier. Now he reached out sudden hands and caught the girl to him violently. "Oh!" she gasped, terrified and outraged at the same time, "Let me g…." The words were cut off in her throat as his violent, seeking lips pressed hungrily against her mouth. She fought with all her strength, but his arms around her were steel and his mouth pressed her head back until the muscles of her neck hurt.

Suddenly, without apparent reason, he released her. The girl staggered back, rubbing the back of her hand against her mouth in a convulsive movement of horror and disgust. McGee was standing motionless, staring in the direction of the door in the corner of the room. She followed his glance.

Lockjaw stood in the open doorway, his head down, like a bull about to charge, and his face was red with anger. "You skunk!" he choked out, and began to walk slowly toward the gambler.

McGee's hand flashed under his coat so fast that the girl did not see it move. She only saw that it had emerged, holding a short-barrelled .32 caliber bulldog revolver which was trained on Lockjaw. "Stand where you are!" the gambler's voice cracked out.

"What you think you're gonna do with that popgun?" Lockjaw asked contemptuously, without interrupting his stride. His own Colts were holstered on his thighs but he made no move toward them. For an instant, the gambler's eyes widened with astonishment and he held his fire.

"Go ahead and shoot," the big awkward figure taunted him. "If you don't know no better than to start poppin' off before a lady. I'm gonna take you apart with my hands!"

CHAPTER 7
MAVERICK BLOOD

BETH HOLCOMB was leaning back on the table against which she had stumbled and for a second she was frozen with astonishment and fear. But now she saw Saint McGee's finger tighten on the trigger and her mind came to life. Her right hand rested on a heavy crystal paper weight and almost without thought she swept it up and threw. The missile struck the gambler's body just as the hammer of the pistol fell, and in the same instant Lockjaw ducked heavily and rushed. The shot, intended for the big man's heart, creased his cheek instead, and Beth saw the blood spurt. But Lockjaw did not check his rush. McGee tried to shoot again, but he had waited too long for the first trigger-pull. Lockjaw's left hand caught his wrist and wrenched it aside just as the small gun exploded.

Then the big man's other hand caught McGee's right arm at the elbow and held it fast. The gambler brought a swift knee up, but Lockjaw's thigh blocked it. An instant later the hand which held McGee's gun-wrist began to twist. It twisted slowly but with the inevitable force and certainty. McGee struggled against it vainly, the sweat standing out on a face grown white and contorted. A strangled cry of agony burst from him and the gun clattered to the floor.

"Lockjaw!" the girl cried. "You mustn't kill him!"

Lockjaw turned a puzzled face toward her. "All right, ma'am," he said regretfully, at length, "have it your way. But he'll shore cause you more trouble than he's worth before he gets through."

He glowered ferociously at the gambler. "Popguns!" he exploded contemptuously. "I'm gonna teach you some manners!" Deliberately, and apparently without effort, he forced his victim back toward the wall. McGee exerted all his hard, sinewy strength to resist him but it was useless. His captor backed him up until his shoulders touched. Then with a bare movement of his ham-like hands he flipped the gambler forward and back. McGee's head cracked against the wall with a sharp thud. When

Lockjaw released him, the man slipped limply to the floor, unconscious.

Lockjaw turned with a pleased smile to the girl. "That'll learn him." he said complacently. "Now we'll just get that there IOU an'...." He started to stoop down, when a voice from the doorway crackled, "Reach for the ceiling, feller, and keep reachin'!"

Lockjaw Johnson straightened and turned deliberately. Two men were in the doorway, six-guns leveled at him. Lockjaw hesitated. A movement at one of the windows caught his eye. Unhurried, he turned his gaze in that direction. A third and fourth man were at the far windows. Their Colts were also ready. A voice spoke from a window behind him. "You aimin' to imitate a swiss cheese, hombre?" it inquired sardonically. "Git them hands high!"

One of the men in the doorway snapped, "Don't auger with him. The head-money pays dead or alive."

Lockjaw put his hands up. "You jaspers think you're smart, don't you?" he remarked, scornfully. It was not an especially brilliant comeback, but it seemed to satisfy Lockjaw.

The man in the doorway disregarded it. "Turn your back," he directed, curtly. Lockjaw turned.

The man walked forward and jammed his gun against his captive's spine. "I'm liftin' your hardware," he warned. "One little quiver and I'll let daylight through you."

Beth Holcomb came to life. "This man has just been protecting me from Saint McGee, Jud," she said. "Please give him back his guns and let him go."

Jud Bronson's jaw dropped. "Sa-ay!" he protested. "Don't you know this is one of the skunks what dry-gulched your uncle?"

"I don't believe it!" the girl told him spiritedly.

Another puncher spoke up. "Shore he is, Miss Beth. He was in that fight down to the river, and later on he pulled Hank off his bronc and got away. We trailed him up here."

"I know that," Beth told him sharply. "But the Five Mavericks didn't kill my uncle. It was somebody else."

Jud Bronson stared at her suspiciously. "What makes you so shore of that, Beth?" he asked sharply.

THE GIRL flushed. She realized that she could give no sensible reason for her belief without telling the basis for her suspicions about Blaze McArthur, and she had a strange reluctance to do that. She told herself that it would be only fair to Blaze to give him a chance to explain first. But in her heart she wondered whether she could steel herself to give her cousin away, even if she knew him guilty. The realization gave her a sense of horror and she told herself immediately that it was not true. Of course she would give him away, rather than condone so dreadful a crime!

She became aware that the punchers were watching her curiously and wondered how much her face had betrayed. She thought quickly, but could think of no answer to Bronson's question.

"Didn't you all see what happened at the river?" she got out finally. "Don't you know that men like that wouldn't shoot anybody in the back!"

Jud Bronson looked relieved and tolerant. Somebody behind

her audibly suppressed a snicker. "I reckon that wouldn't hardly pass for proof in court," Bronson remarked, "so we'll just take this rattler in, regardless."

"What's the use of takin' him in, Jud?" objected the man in the doorway. "Let's string him up and get it over with."

Murmurs of approval came from the men. Saint McGee stirred, groaned a little and sat up, holding his head. Nobody paid any attention to him.

"We couldn't claim the reward then," Bronson returned.

"How come? The poster says dead or alive. It don't make no specifications about how he comes to be dead."

"Jud's right," another puncher put in. "The law's full of tricks. They might hold out on us."

The girl said desperately, "You're not going to hang him or take him to jail, either! You forget that this is my ranch now. I order you to let him go."

Bronson looked at her. "There's something funny here," he muttered.

Saint McGee said suddenly, "You bet there's something funny! She was hiding him in that other room here when I came in. I discovered him and when he went for me, she threw that paper weight at me and spoiled my aim."

The girl said, *"Oh!"* as though she could not believe her ears.

Lockjaw snarled accusingly. "I told you you oughter let me kill him!"

"This gets funnier and funnier," Jud Bronson commented grimly.

"If you'll take my advice," McGee said evenly, "you'll shoot him right now. Nobody'll have any question about the reward then."

"Now you're talkin'!" exclaimed the cowboy in the doorway, raising his Colt. Lockjaw said, "Make a good job of it. If you don't hit me right I'm shore gonna twist this pole-cat's neck!" His wooden, horse-long features took on an expression of angry determination as his big, barrel-chested body tensed. McGee backed hastily away from him.

The man in the doorway thumbed back his hammer. "I ain't likely to miss," he said grimly.

Beth Holcomb cried out, "Why, it's murder!" and threw herself desperately in front of Lockjaw. Then things began to happen with startling suddenness. Lockjaw crouched and rushed for Saint McGee. The latter turned like a bob-cat and tried to twist away but a long arm shot out and caught him by the neck, jerked him back.

The man in the doorway thumbed a quick shot as Lockjaw left the cover of Beth's body, but the cowpuncher was embarrassed by the fear of hitting the girl and his bullet went wide. Before he could shoot again, Lockjaw, pushing the gambler ahead of him as a shield, was on him. Unable to shoot, the cowboy raised his gun-barrel and struck for the big man's head. The latter ducked, took the blow on his shoulder. His free hand grabbed the gun, wrenched it loose from the man's hand.

The other men, who had climbed in through the windows as soon as Lockjaw had been disarmed, were dancing around trying for a shot, but seeing that that was impossible they rushed in from all sides, guns clubbed, aiming for Lockjaw.

Without shifting his hand, Lockjaw smashed the butt of the captured Colt onto its owner's head. McGee he sent hurtling at the legs of one of the punchers who were rushing him. The man went down with a crash. Lockjaw jumped for another. A six-gun blasted under his nose and something hot ripped across his ribs, then his Colt fell, missing the gunman's head by a bare half inch, smashing at his collar bone. Under the force of that terrific blow the man went down like a pole-axed steer.

Then the barrel of Jud Bronson's Colt slashed across Lockjaw's skull and the light went out for him, too.

SAINT McGEE, his pale bright eyes flaring maniacally, twisted to his feet, his hands flashing for the fallen six-gun of the man who had tripped over his hurtling body. He got it, leveled it at Lockjaw's unconscious form, his mouth twisted in a snarl of deadly fury. "Now, you…."

The bellow of another gun blasted his words. The cocked revolver flew from his hand, jerked with the shock of its own report and slammed into a corner. Its wild slug hit the ceiling.

Doc Grimson's voice snapped and crackled like a gap-jumping spark. "Hold it! The first man who makes a wrong move rides to hell. Grab air, you hombres, and hang on!"

The men who were still on their feet froze under the deadly urgency of that command, shot startled glances at the window where luminous gray eyes blazed at them and a still-smoking Colt seemed to menace each man individually. From another window, a dryer, less urgent voice spoke up. "We'd ruther not kill you boys, but there ain't no more of us goin' to shoot for a man's gun-hand."

A big-shouldered young man, with red-gold hair, appeared suddenly in the doorway. He held twin six-guns in his hands.

There was a staccato thudding on the carpet as the men in the room dropped their weapons and got their hands up in a hurry.

For a long moment there was silence, then Beth Holcomb said "Oh!" in a weak voice and crumpled up on the floor.

Lance stepped to her quickly, bent down, his eyes searching for a sign of some wound. Doc Grimson was in the room like a flash. He bent over the girl, while Charlie Parr and Flint Maddox herded the punchers and McGee into a corner.

"Fainted," Doc pronounced briefly. "Be around in a minute." He went to Lockjaw and bent over him swiftly, supple, delicate fingers searching his body.

"Bullet slashed along his ribs," was his verdict. "Aside from the gash where the gentleman caressed his head with a six-gun, there doesn't seem to be anything else."

A faint thunder of hard-ridden horses drifted through the window. As one man, the four Mavericks raised their heads, tensing.

"Friend McArthur," observed Charlie Parr drily.

"Pretty quick trailin'," nodded Flint Maddox, in the manner of a man who delivers a fair, judicial judgment.

Doc Grimson said quietly, "Get moving! Lance, you and Flint take Lockjaw."

They moved quickly, smoothly, efficiently. A moment later the barrel-chested man's two hundred and twenty-five pounds of big bone and solid muscle had disappeared gently through a window, and Doc Grimson, the last of the quintette to leave was poised with one foot on the sill.

"Your guns will be under the window," he said quietly to the group huddled in the corner. "Don't come for them too quickly. As for you"—he singled out Saint McGee,—"I don't like your looks nor your ways. We may meet again."

The gambler's lips drew back from his thin lips. "When we do," he snarled, "I'm going to kill you so dead that you'll stink in hell!"

Doc Grimson smiled faintly as he slipped through the window. The hoof-beats of the sheriff's posse were a staccato thunder in front of the house.

CHAPTER 8
LAW THROWDOWN!

THE MID-AFTERNOON sun beat hot on the mesa top and sent metallic vibrations hammering back and forth from the rocks, the twisted lava formations, the ravines and gullies of the badlands below.

Lance Clayton, at post as lookout behind a sparse tangle of Joshua trees, watched the half-hearted casting about of the sheriff's posse lead them farther toward the back-trail to town. Some miles away another posse appeared, angling in through one of the maze of twisting arroyos. The two groups met, pulled leg-weary horses to a halt, and after a short parley turned as though by common consent onto the home trail.

Lance crawled back to where the others were trying to find comfort in the sketchy shade of some cholla cactus.

"Looks like the boys have given up," he reported cheerfully.

" 'Bout time," grunted Charlie Parr.

"What's next, Doc?"

"Stick right here," clipped Doc. "Our job's not done yet, by a long shot. Somewhere in this county are five murderers who are wearing our brand."

"We'll vent that—plenty!" Lance said grimly. "All we're aching for is a chance at 'em. But they can sure cover their trail—"

Doc said, "Watching the sheriff's boys work out for this seat up here gives me an idea. We've got to find a day-time hideout near town. With glasses, we can check up pretty well on the comings and goings. Blaze McArthur needs watching. Maybe we'll find out something. It's about the best we can do. We can't go into town—we can't even be seen around the countryside. This whole county has our descriptions and is watching for us."

Lance said, "Sounds like a long time no have fun."

"Doc's right, though," Charlie Parr agreed. "We can't fight a whole county. I'm guessin' there's enough lead saved up for us in the town of Sageville to sink us all clear through to China."

Lockjaw said, "I got to go to town." Charlie Parr looked at him with irritation. "You can't go to town," he snapped. "Want to get your fool self lynched?" Lockjaw looked apologetic. "I got to, Charlie," he repeated.

Charlie looked outraged. "There's a jawhead for you!" he exclaimed.

Doc Grimson smiled. "Why do you have to go to town, Lockjaw," he asked.

"He's still got that there slip—the skunk!" Lockjaw answered, evidently relieved at avoiding an argument with Charlie.

"Slip?" Charlie roared. "Who said anything about a slip? What slip—and who's got it?"

"Why, the IOU," Lockjaw explained uncomfortably. "You see, I was about to get it for her, after the way she stood by me. But them fellers came. I got to get it for her."

Charlie Parr controlled himself with difficulty. While his face grew apoplectic and he fought to find his voice, Doc Grimson interposed, "I reckon you'd better tell us the whole story, Lockjaw," he said easily.

"Didn't I tell you?" Lockjaw looked surprised. "Why, you see, it was this way." And he repeated what had happened and his version of the conversation between McGee and Beth. "So I got to go in an' take it off him," he ended simply. They tried to explain to him that it would be better to get at it some other way—what he proposed was impossible.

"But he's goin' to make trouble for her!" Lockjaw insisted.

"Maybe," Doc Grimson told him, "but you can't do any good by going into that town, Lockjaw. Even if you got this McGee, you'd never get out alive. It wouldn't do the girl any good."

CHARLIE PARR looked like a man who has just remembered something. "By Gravy!" he jerked out. "I knew that feller's face was familiar. That there's Saint McGee—used to be house-gambler down at Smoky Joe's in Tularosa! Remember, Doc?"

Doc threw back his head in surprised recollection. "You're right!" he agreed. "He hasn't changed much. Things were happening so fast in there that I never thought of it."

"Who is this McGee?" Lance asked.

"Gambler and killer," Doc Grimson explained briefly. "And plenty poison. Fast with a gun, crooked as a rattler lying in the sun, and doesn't give warning when he strikes. He ran a crooked game in Tularosa but it wasn't easy to prove even if anybody'd had had the nerve to try. One feller did, and he died. McGee shoots just once from a small shoulder gun—places it either in the heart or between the eyes. Most generally the eyes."

"Is that why they call him Saint?" Flint Maddox inquired sardonically.

Doc smiled. "No, he got that name because he doesn't smoke or drink and because once, when he began to get unpopular, he took to going to church. It was a smart move and it let him hang on a good while. Finally, though, a committee of citizens asked him to get out. They admitted they didn't have anything on him but told him the climate wouldn't be healthy for him from then on."

"I knew he was a crook!" Lockjaw exclaimed. "Wouldn't nobody but a crook go kissin' a girl like that without she wanted him to. I'm goin' to take him apart!"

Charlie Parr groaned. "You're goin' to get a slug in that dumb head of your'n," he said. "After that, they'll take your body out and cut it up and feed it to the hawgs."

Lockjaw got to his feet. He looked excessively uncomfortable. "Well," he membled, "I guess I'll take a little *pasear.*"

"You goin' to town?" Charlie Parr flared.

Lockjaw shifted on his feet, awkwardly, put his hands behind his back, apparently found the position uncomfortable, weaved them about helplessly in front of him and said, "Aw, now, Charlie—if I don't git there in a hurry that snake's goin' to do somethin' with that IOU."

Charlie Par rolled his eyes to heaven. "Go on!" he shouted in disgusted wrath. "Go on and git your fool self killed. Nobody's goin' to worry about it."

Lockjaw looked deeply dejected. "She shore tried to help me out," he muttered, turning stubbornly toward his horse.

"What's the matter with you? You in love with this girl?" Charlie fired at him, pinning a last hope in ridicule.

Lockjaw turned back and his long, dumb, wooden features took on an expression of fatuous happiness. "You'd ought to have seed the way she smiled at me," he said. "Put her hands right on my shoulders, too!"

Charlie Parr lay back with a groan of despair. "Sweet on her!" he announced unbelievingly to a faintly astonished sky. "Sweet on her! Of all the danged, bat-eared, ignorant, jaw-headed fools…."

But Lockjaw was already in the saddle and riding away. The bloom of joyous self-congratulation still glowing on his face.

When he had gone, their laughter lasted only a minute.

"We can't let him go alone," Doc Grimson said. "We'll have to go with him."

Lance and Flint agreed instantly. Charlie Parr looked from one to the other and then shrugged his shoulders with an air of resigned irritation. "All right—all right," he snapped. "Make fools of yourself. Me—I've naturally got to foller after the mule-headed son, but that ain't no reason why you have to. Two long-eared jacks on the road is plenty!"

Nobody paid any attention to that. "Maybe it would be better to foller along behind him than to go with him," Lance suggested, addressing Doc.

"I think you're right," the latter answered thoughtfully. "And when we get toward town we'd better split up and come in from different sides. Have more chance of getting by without being recognized that way. Lockjaw'll head straight for Saint McGee's place—wherever that is. We'll time it so as to arrive at the same time."

They agreed on that.

LOCKJAW, MEANWHILE, rode on ahead. He tried to keep himself from feeling hurt because the boys wouldn't come with him. He had always come with them, wherever they wanted to go. Now, just about the first time he wanted to do something…. Still, he was kind of glad they were going to stay out of town. They might get themselves killed in there. After all, the girl hadn't tried to save *their* lives. Then the beatific memory of the way Beth had put her hands on his shoulders and looked up at him returned, and he rode the rest of the trail in a sort of roseate fog. No girl as pretty and nice as that had ever paid any attention to him. Of course, he guessed it was just friendliness…. Still and all, there had been something in her eyes…. He still felt dazed when he thought of it.

Automatically, he watched the trail ahead and at the sides,

but he was too much preoccupied to pay much attention to the trail behind him. He didn't know that back there the other four Mavericks rode, keeping him in sight but not showing themselves much.

Once he got a glimpse of some men riding ahead of him. They appeared for a second on a rise and then disappeared. They looked as though they had come in from the badlands at an angle to him. He didn't pay much attention to them, because he judged that they had not seen him. Automatically he noticed that one of them wore a red shirt and rode a sorrel horse with white stockings.

After that he met nobody until he got into town, just at sunset. A man or two looked at him curiously but he rode placidly on. Pretty soon, he figured, he'd have to ask somebody where this Saint McGee's place was.

He figured that a fancy gambler, like this McGee, would be sure to have his hang-out in some saloon on the main drag, so he automatically set his course down the middle of the wide street which formed Sageville's principal thoroughfare.

A couple of punchers strolled out of the first saloon door he came to and he leaned down and addressed one of them. "Say, pardner, where does this Saint McGee hang out?

The cowboy looked at him curiously and seemed in no hurry to reply. "I'm lookin' for him," said Lockjaw patiently, by way of explanation.

"Stranger here, I reckon," the puncher remarked, owlishly.

"Kind of," Lockjaw admitted.

"Well, I tell you, I can put you on the trail to McGee's place so you can't miss it. You see that big-fronted buildin' up the street with the sign that says 'Crystal Palace?'" Lockjaw looked up and nodded. "Well, you go on until you get right up to it, then you turn right into the door, and there you are. That there's McGee's place. He runs it, an' I reckon he's right there now."

"I'm right obliged," Lockjaw told him courteously, and gathered his horse to go on.

A man came out of a nearby doorway and stopped short at the sight of Lockjaw, giving vent to an oath of astonishment. Lockjaw caught the glitter of a star on the man's vest and instantly recognized Sheriff Blaze McArthur. Lockjaw went for his guns.

The sheriff went for his at the same instant, so the only advantage he had was that almost anybody was faster on the draw than Lockjaw—and Blaze McArthur was faster than most men. Once Lockjaw's Colts were leveled in those rock-like hands of his, they could deal death with deadlier accuracy than could the guns of even Doc Grimson. But Lockjaw needed time to get unlimbered and into action. His ham-like paws had just gripped the worn walnut butts of his guns, when McArthur's came flashing up with hammers thumbed back. The sheriff had plenty of time.

And then something exploded in the back of his head. His knees crumpled. The Colt, falling, belched flame in the twilight, its slug kicking up a spurt of dust in the roadway.

The two punchers, who had directed Lockjaw, were not too full of red-eye to duck for cover. They saw only that a tall, youngish looking man with big shoulders had laid his six-gun

87

barrel against the back of the sheriff's head. After that the street was confusion. A deputy came running, gun in hand, from the sheriff's office. The mounted man's right Colt sent him spinning, clutching at his shoulder. Three riders raced down the street. One of them caught the reins of the big man's horse and an instant later the four were off down the street in a haze of dust and gun-fire.

"The Mavericks! The Mavericks!" someone was yelling. "Get 'em! It's the Mavericks!"

Men poured out of nearby saloons, jumped for horses that stood along the hitchracks. An excited crowd of citizens milled in the street.

"One of 'em's on foot," yelled the man who had spoken to Lockjaw, realizing suddenly what had happened. "Come on! He went this way."

The crowd swarmed to the entrance between two buildings through which Lance Clayton had disappeared, shouting, "Get him before he gets to his bronc! Kill him!"

CHAPTER 9
MAVERICK MASQUERADERS

LANCE, WHEN he had separated from the others, had ridden hard to get into town first. He wanted to examine the lay of the land, find out where McGee's place was, and try to make some plan which would help Lockjaw accomplish his purpose. He had an idea that the others had followed in only to be able to lend the big fellow a hand when trouble started, but Lance knew that that would not be enough.

As long as McGee held the paper which Lockjaw wanted, just so long would the long-faced, stolid Maverick continue to run his neck into danger. The way to stop him was to help him succeed, and Lance, the youngest of the five, alone had the necessary optimism to think the thing might be possible.

He had come into town by back ways and, more adroit than Lockjaw, had inquired his way of an old Mexican who looked about half blind. He had left his horse in back of the Crystal Palace and gone on foot to intercept Lockjaw, arriving just in time to spoil Blaze McArthur's aim.

Now, with the shouts of the crowd in his ears, he went swiftly back to where he had left his mount—swiftly, but without running and with little appearance of haste. He knew that he had time. The sorrel stallion would outrun anything in town, he felt sure.

Opposite the rear entrance to McGee's saloon he paused. A quick glance over his shoulder assured him that the mob had not yet found his trail. He could get to his horse in a dozen strides—and be away before anyone even sighted him. But another idea occurred to him. He had come in to help Lockjaw get a paper from McGee. The gambler's place was here. Why not go through with it? The last place in the world that anybody would look for him would be right here in the Crystal Palace saloon. On impulse, he reached out and tried the rear door of the saloon. It opened. He stepped inside.

Lance had no sooner gotten in when he realized that he had

made a mistake. They might find his horse—probably would. When they did, the search would center here. In any case, he was in the worst possible place. McGee had seen him, would recognize him in an instant. If he had to shoot it out with the gambler or any of his henchmen, there wouldn't be much chance of his fighting his way out of town alive. And McGee was dangerous—poison dangerous, if Lance's guess was right. Doc Grimson and Charlie Parr did not talk of many men in that tone of mingled distaste and respect.

These thoughts raced through his mind as he stood just inside the door, and for a moment, despite the pursuit outside, he was impelled to turn back. But something stubborn in him held him there.

He found himself in a long corridor, dimly lighted by one lantern affixed to the wall. Through the wooden partition at the left he could hear sounds of voices, the clatter of glasses and the click of chips which told him that the main room of the saloon and gambling house was there. A door, let into that wall at the end of the corridor, evidently gave into this room. By it was a flight of wooden steps which he judged led to rooms above. The wall at his right had a number of doors in it, opening, evidently, into small, individual rooms. One of them, he thought, might be McGee's private office. He tiptoed softly down the hall.

When he came to the first door a pencil of light shown through the crack at the bottom, but when he listened, he could detect no movement inside. While he hesitated before it a door opened upstairs; there was a sound of voices, and feet began to

Lance laughed and took a step toward her. "Better shoot before it's too late..." he said.

descend the stairs. If he were caught here now.... A pair of trim, booted legs appeared to his vision on the stairs. Quickly, softly, he opened the door to the room and stepped inside.

A GIRL sat there, before a crude pine dressing table with a cracked mirror, looking at him with anger in her eyes. She started to speak, but Lance held a quick finger to his lips. Her eyes fell on the gun he held at the side of his leg, traveled slowly up to his face again, and widened with a sudden emotion which did not, somehow, seem to be fear. She had been making up her face, now she dropped her lipstick and bent quickly down to recover it.

The sound of steps in the hallway separated at the main door of the saloon, one pair coming down the hall. Lance felt behind his back, found a key in the door and turned it softly. "I'll have time to get out the window, anyway," he thought. Then he saw that the room was windowless.

The steps came up to the door, passed it in unbroken rhythm, and a moment later Lance heard the rear door open and shut. He let out his breath in a sigh of relief.

"Not very noisy, are you?" the girl commented tartly. She had black hair and eyes and a pertly twisted mouth and the tinselled bodice of her evening gown displayed plump shoulders and a good deal of bosom. "What are you doin' here?" she demanded.

Lance grinned suddenly. He wished he knew! "You got me," he acknowledged. "If you know the answer, tell it to me."

"Just around seein' the sights and dropped in by mistake, is that it?" she demanded sarcastically.

Lance grinned. "I couldn't call this a mistake!" he grinned, his tone of voice complimentary.

The girl cocked a cynical eye at him and turned back toward the mirror. She rubbed rouge on her lower lip and nibbled at it with the upper, spreading it smooth.

"Why don't you sit down and make yourself easy?" she invited, indicating the single remaining chair. "Hang the hardware on the wall before it gets your hand all weighted down."

Lance sat down and slipped his gun back into its holster. The girl gave a final straightening touch to her hair and then reached down and lifted her skirt on the side away from Lance, apparently to straighten her garter. When she straightened up again she held a small, nickle-plated derringer in her hand, pointed at Lance.

"Put your hands up, Mr. Clayton," she said crisply.

Lance looked at her. "You're pretty smart," he said at length, slowly. "How'd you know who I was?"

"You'd be surprised how much I know. But don't let that keep you from putting your hands up."

"Suppose I didn't feel like goin' to all that trouble?" he suggested, his eyes beginning to dance.

"You think I won't shoot?" the girl demanded. "Maybe you don't know how much money there is on your head or how high I'll stand with the boss for gettin' you."

"I been hearin' about this reward," Lance said pleasantly. "How much is it, anyway?"

"Three thousand dollars in gold!" the girl told him tartly. "Three thousand on every one of the five of you—fifteen thousand for the lot. No bargain prices; cash on delivery, dead or alive. And don't think I can't hit you with this thing, either."

Lance saw that, in fact, the small, plump hand which held the derringer was entirely steady. It looked as if she wouldn't miss.

He smiled. "I'm bettin' you could drill me dead center," he

said. "Let me have a look at that thing, will you? That's a pretty one." He held out his hand.

The girl drew back sharply. "No you don't!" she warned, setting her lips firmly. "Make another move like that and I'll let you have it."

"No, you won't," Lance told her lazily. "You know why you won't?"

"You tell me," the girl snapped at him, "and I'll show you!"

"I'll tell you, all right," Lance grinned in his friendly fashion. "It's because you couldn't kill anybody for money. That's not your sort. You might shoot somebody that was tryin' to hurt you, or if you got mad enough at 'em—I dunno. But money—no. There's mighty little you'd do for money."

For just an instant the girl's black eyes wavered, then they hardened. "You just try something and see," she said, tightening her grip on the derringer.

"I'm goin' to," Lance assured her calmly. "I'm goin' to get up and come over and take that little gun away from you, and you won't do anything about it, because you know I wouldn't ever try to harm you, no matter what happened. I could just get up and walk out of here but that's not what I want to do. I'm plumb curious to see that nice little gun, an' I'm even more curious to see whether you'll shoot or not." He got up out of his chair.

THE GIRL'S eyes widened. "You—you wouldn't do it," she said in a voice which sounded a little weak. "You got too much sense!"

Lance laughed and took a step toward her, saying, "Better

shoot before it's too late. Three thousand dollars is a lot of money."

"Oh!" the girl cried, outraged. She slapped the derringer down suddenly on the dressing table, whirled and stamped off into a corner of the room. "You're a fool!" she said furiously.

Lance picked up the derringer and walked over to her. He rubbed the muzzle gently across her bare back. The girl shivered a little at the caress of the steel. "It's mighty pretty," Lance told her. "Almost pretty enough for you—and lots too pretty for me. So you take it. You might get to thinking of that three thousand dollars and I'd shore hate to think I was to blame for your losin' 'em."

The girl's shoulders shook a little and a small giggle broke from her. "Can't you be serious about anything?" she asked. "That's important money."

She turned and snatched the gun from Lance's hand. "It isn't loaded, anyway," she said, making a face at him. "I've got the wrong kind of temper to be carryin' a loaded gun."

"Lady," Lance informed her, "you ain't got the wrong kind of anything. Everything about you is plumb right."

"Thanks. You're not so bad yourself," the girl told him with sudden simplicity. "I've heard plenty about you, without believin' too much of what I heard. But say, when you walked in here tonight, lookin' as calm as a parson at a church sociable, why, I was ready to believe everything I'd heard and then some. And since then I been learin' right along. What's the matter with you—you tired of livin' or just born dumb?"

"You sound like this place was dangerous."

"Yeah—" drily, "that's the way I meant to sound. I guess you don't know much about Saint McGee, or Flicker Evans, or Monk Slade. Or did you think they was all out callin' somewheres?"

"Bad medicine, are they?" Lance asked softly.

"Listen, Handsome, you think you're pretty good, but you ain't good enough for them. Why any one of 'em would eat you for breakfast an' then holler for ham an' eggs."

"You sure make 'em sound right interestin'. It reminds me that I been honin' to talk with your boss. Couldn't you get him in here for me?"

The girl stared indignantly. "What do you take me for?" she snapped. "You think I'm the kind to double-cross a man like that?"

"I reckon you don't understand. You think I want to take some kind of advantage," Lance told her gravely. "I don't. I'm not goin' to hurt him at all, unless he wants it bad enough—an' if it comes to that I'll let him go for his gun first. I give you my word to that."

The girl stared at him as though he were crazy. "By golly!" she marveled after a moment, "I believe you mean it!"

"I mean it all right."

She shook her head decisively. "The answer is no," she told him flatly.

"Why? You afraid he'll get hurt?"

She stared. *"He* wouldn't get hurt—not if you kept your word. But you would, and then I would. He'd kill me once for havin' a man in here and twice because it was you."

"Jealous, is he?"

"Yes, he's jealous," she told him pertly. "Do you blame him?" And before he could reply she said, "Go on, now, Handsome— before he takes a notion to come in here. I oughtn't to have let you stay so long, only I'm weak that way. Run! Shoo! And don't come back. I don't want to see you hurt."

LANCE THOUGHT fast. He wanted that IOU. If only he could persuade this girl to get him alone with McGee! He said, "He's jealous of you but you're not supposed to be jealous of him, is that it."

The girl said tartly, "There's no one for me to be jealous about."

"Then I suppose you wouldn't have minded if he had got to marry Beth Holcomb."

The girl's eyes snapped angrily. "He doesn't go to see that little—that little—"

Lance said hastily, "Funny he was out there this mornin' then, tryin' to kiss her and gettin' his face slapped."

"You're lying! How could you know that?"

"A partner of mine was there, hiding in the next room. McGee tried to get her to marry him and when she wouldn't he lost his head and threatened to do something to her—'break her,' I think he said. That's what I want to see him about."

The girl came at him, blazing. "Get out of here," she stormed, her eyes lancing fury. "Do you hear? Get out! I'll call Saint McGee to take care of *you*—I'll call Flicker and Monk; you hear me? I'll have this place after you like a pack of wolves, you yellow coyote! Git! Go on, git!"

Lance shrugged and turned to the door. He had lost. Better get to his horse and ride for it.

"Wait!" the girl's voice was husky with anger but it had calmed a little.

He turned again, staring, and she stood with her hands clenched, her bosom heaving. "I'm goin' to tell you," she half whispered, furiously, "I'll give him away to you. I'll teach him how to lie to me, the skunk! Listen, an hour or two ago I heard him talking to Flicker and Monk. It was about a girl they were going to take—kidnap. I heard him say, 'Don't worry about that—I'll tame her. She'll never talk!'"

"He told me it was the little Eastman girl—they were going to make her dad pay to get her back. He said she wouldn't be hurt. I believed him—the liar! Now I know it's that Holcomb girl. He's taking her because he wants her—damn him!"

Lance's eyes blazed. "When are they goin' after her?" he demanded brusquely.

"Tonight," she told him, her eyes narrowed. "I heard him say, 'have the bunch ready before midnight.'"

Lance pricked up his ears. "What bunch?" he asked softly.

The girl looked sobered. "I won't tell you that," she said, after a moment's hesitation.

"Wasn't he lying to you?" whispered Lance, hating himself. "Isn't he goin' to throw you over for another girl?"

The girl glared at him. "You're a devil!" she breathed. "Well— all right. I guess you know anyway—but if you ever tell anybody I told you…."

"I won't. I give you my word on it," Lance said, and held his breath.

"They're the gang that have been signin' things with your sign—the Five Mavericks," she said, almost too low to be heard.

Lance expelled his held breath in a long, soft sigh. "Where do they hang out?" he asked, quickly.

"I don't know; somewhere up in the badlands. If you ever let it out that I told.... They wouldn't just kill me—they'd—they'd torture me... until I died...."

"Don't worry about that," Lance told her softly, and stopped short. The door to the main saloon had opened and closed. Footsteps, brisk, self-assured, were coming down the corridor.

The girl's face went deathly white under her rouge. "It's Saint!" she whispered. "He's coming in here!"

CHAPTER 10
LANCE BAITS A TRAP

L ANCE'S HAND went to the butts of his guns.

"No, no!" she pled desperately. "In there, quick!" Her gesture pointed to a sort of cupboard, built out from the wall, curtained in front and filled with dance-hall costumes.

Lance hesitated, then moved swiftly, cat-like, and disappeared behind the curtains. This was no time for a showdown. Besides, he owed it to the girl to keep his presence unknown.

The curtains had scarcely ceased quivering after his passage when the gambler's hand was on the doorknob.

"What's the matter, Kate?" he rapped out. "Open the door!"

She moved to it quickly and unlocked it.

"What's the idea of having it locked?" McGee demanded suspiciously.

"Some fool drunk wandered in here a little while ago," the girl told him. "I locked it to keep him from coming back."

"Why didn't you let me know?"

"Oh, I handled him. He was harmless."

"You don't look like he had been. What's the matter with you—kind of peaked, aren't you."

"Yeah, I've got a headache—been feelin' kind of bad all day."

McGee flicked his wide-eyed glance around the room. When he spoke again the note of suspicion had left his tone. He asked idly, "Who was this drunk? Someone from around here?"

"No," the girl told him, "It was some pilgrim that blew in here today—he didn't know any better."

"They don't know anything," the gambler remarked easily. "I see you've got your gun handy, though." He reached out casually as though to take it up, but carelessly let it fall to the floor. The girl stooped swiftly to pick it up but McGee caught her shoulder with a forestalling gesture.

"My dear!" he reproached her. "You mustn't let me forget my manners." There was the lightest possible touch of mockery in his voice.

The girl watched him with widened eyes and a countenance gone suddenly paler as he stooped, stretching his left hand toward the derringer. She saw his right hand move casually toward the lapel of his coat as he did so, saw it flash out holding a gun, watched him start to whirl toward the clothes closet.

"Hold it there, McGee!" Lance's voice cracked out warningly. "I've got you covered."

The gambler froze, his crouching pivot half completed.

"Drop your gun on the floor and stand up with your hands over your head."

For an almost imperceptible instant, McGee hesitated, then he did as he was directed.

Lance stepped out of the closet. "Pretty smart, McGee," he said lightly. "How'd you guess I was there?"

The gambler's face was impassive, his pale eyes cold.

"Maybe you think you don't smell horse," he answered sardonically. "Or maybe you think a lady's dressing room generally smells horse."

He flicked his gaze to the girl. "You should have said your drunk was a wandering puncher," he remarked gently. "You'd have had more chance of fooling me."

The girl called Kate shivered. She tried to speak but her tongue clove to the roof of her mouth.

"Give the lady credit, McGee," Lance advised him, still in his ironic tone. "She thought of the only way possible to warn you without getting a bullet through you both."

The words seemed like a flow of fresh water through the dance-girl's fear-parched body. They brought her to life. "It's about the credit I expected," she said tartly. "Saint always believes he's the only one who can think fast."

McGee's eyes grew narrow. He shifted his glance rapidly from one to the other.

"Are you trying to tell me," he asked of the girl, "that you didn't talk up because…."

"What would you have done, with a gun in your back and one of the Five Mavericks behind it?" she blazed at him by way of response. "I notice you've got your hands pretty high, right now!"

"I'm glad to hear that was the reason," Saint McGee said softly. "I hope I don't ever have cause to suspect that there was any other reason."

THE WORDS were spoken without emphasis, gently, but Lance felt his backbone grow cold as he listened to them. And because he felt fear in him, he got angry.

"Your specialty seems to be threatening women, McGee," he rapped out. "Turn your back and let me get over my business with you, before I get tempted to ventilate you."

McGee's eyes narrowed. "Pretty gallant talk for an hombre who's just been holding a gun on a woman," he commented, watching the other man hard.

Lance saw that he had make a mistake but he was enough of a poker player not to change expression. "That was necessary," he said shortly. "At least I don't try to blackmail them with fake IOUs."

The gambler looked suddenly venomous. "And just what is this business you have with me?" he asked.

"I want that IOU. Goin' to produce it, or am I goin' to fan you for it?"

"You're goin' to fan me for it," the gambler told him coolly. "I destroyed it within ten minutes after I left the house."

"You ought to have," Lance told him gently. "That's what you mean. Your kind doesn't tear up anything there might be a profit in, even when it's evidence against you. Turn around."

McGee looked at him a second, his face devoid of expression. Then he said, "There's no need to. What you want is in my right vest pocket. Shall I give it to you, or are you afraid to let me get a hand down."

Lance laughed. "I'm afraid of more than that," he said, mockingly. "I'm afraid you must have something else in your pockets that you don't want me to see. So turn around anyhow."

McGee shrugged and turned. Lance felt first in the vest pocket he had indicated and drew out a slip of paper. He saw at once that it was an IOU, signed by Fred Holcomb, for $22,500.

"Well, well! Here it is!" he said mockingly. "You know when your bluff's been called all right, don't you, Saint?"

He put the slip of paper in his own pocket and then fanned the gambler thoroughly. The result, aside from some odds and ends, was three packets of money, two of them for twenty-five hundred dollars, and one for five thousand, according to the figures written on a brown paper band around each packet.

Lance whistled. "Carry plenty with you, don't you?" he commented. "I expect the boys will be right pleased."

He was about to put the bills into his pocket when a similarity between the figures on the brown paper bands and those on the IOU struck him. He backed off toward the lamp, to examine them.

"Don't get encouraged to move, Saint," he said coldly, "I'm watchin' you."

The gambler laughed shortly. "I'm not a fool," he said. "Several of you are going to find that out before you're through."

Lance's eyes widened as he compared the figures. The "2s" and the "5s" were exactly alike, made in a peculiar way which made the "2" look like a "z" but the oughts of the IOU were definitely different from those of the bills.

"You skunk!" he said contemptuously, "You aren't even a very good crook. You thought all zeros looked alike, didn't you? You made a big mistake, McGee—one that may hang you!"

Lance had remembered Lockjaw's report of how Beth Holcomb had said her uncle had written only part of the figures on the IOU, and it wasn't hard for him to conclude that an IOU for $225 had been raised to $22,500. It was easy to guess, too, after what the girl, Kate, had told him, that the money he held had been taken from the dead body of Fred Holcomb.

A thrill of excitement ran through him. This little excursion on Lockjaw's account had resulted in plenty! He had not only solved the mystery of the impersonation of the Five Mavericks, but he held in his hands evidence that could be made to stick, with Beth Holcomb's testimony, in any court in the land. Moreover, they had the chance now to nab the whole gang red-handed, in an attempt to kidnap the girl!

Kate's voice broke in on his excited thinking. *"Hurry,* Lance," she cried out suddenly, like a woman who can contain herself no longer. "Somebody may come in here any minute. Hurry!"

He stared at her. Her face looked strained, frantic.

"Oh, don't look at me like that," she broke out at once. "Don't you see what you've done to me? He doesn't believe me. The fool doesn't even believe the truth when he hears it! He's goin' to kill me. It's written all over his face. You've got to take me away from here. Lance! You've got to—do you hear?" The words tumbled from her lips frantically.

She went toward Lance with her hands held out, pleading, apparently beside herself.

"Wait!" Lance said sharply, seeing a slight tension come into McGee's body.

"No!" she cried, "Come *now!*"

And then, like a flash, she was on Lance's gun-arm, knocking it aside. *"Now*, Saint!" she screamed, hanging to the gun-arm like grim death, "Now!"

M c GEE'S WHIRL was lightning. As Lance's left hand flashed for its holstered gun, the gambler's fist drove squarely between his eyes. The left gun came up, wavering. Lance's mind, for that brief second, was nothing but a blinding flash of light. The edge of McGee's rigid palm slashed down viciously on Lance's forearm, the hand of which held the freed gun. Involuntarily, Lance's fingers relaxed and the Colt fell. Like a whiplash McGee's hand struck for it, caught it before it hit the floor.

An instant later, the gambler's gun was hard against Lance's ribs, and McGee's voice was harsh and deadly in his ears, "Drop the other one!"

There was nothing to do. The other gun was muffled by Kate's body; he could not fire it. He eased the hammer down, let the Colt fall to the floor. The girl stooped and picked it.

The rear door of the saloon opened and closed. The sound of two men's footsteps were in the hall.

"Get your hands high," McGee commanded Lance, then he raised his voice. "That you, Flicker—that you, Monk?"

"Yeah," was the simultaneous response.

"Come in here, then."

The door opened and the pair came in. His first glance at them told Lance all he wanted to know. Kate had scarcely exaggerated when she spoke of these two. The man who must have been Monk Slade was a stocky, bow-legged specimen, with the face of an ape and the shoulders of one, too. Immense those shoulders were, so tremendously muscled that they appeared almost to be humped. From them hung heavy, powerful arms, with the gorilla curve and length in them. For the rest he had shortish, bow legs, small, evil eyes, and a wide, brutal, toothy mouth. He might have been funny if he had not been so obviously a killer.

The other, Flicker Evans, was a small, wiry, nervous man, with what looked like only half a face, so narrow and twisted was it. A scar, running to one ear, plucked at the corner of his mouth, lifting it in a continual shaggle-toothed snarl. His narrowed, lashless eyes blinked continually and then popped suddenly open, to stay that way for long, staring moments. His hands were slender, long-fingered, and moved, when they moved at all, in quick nervous flashes, like a ground-squirrel's paws. Low on his thighs were strapped a pair of six-guns in shiny holsters.

The pair stood and looked at Lance, their eyes gleaming. Then Monk Slade guffawed. He didn't say anything. He just stood there with his hands on his hips and threw his head back and laughed. His big teeth showed yellow and his little round black eyes almost disappeared. But Lance knew he was watching him all the time he laughed.

Flicker Evans grinned like a weasel. "Caught yourself somethin' pretty, didn't you, Boss?" he remarked. His hands had dropped casually to the butts of his guns—casually but with a flicking rapidity which spoke volumes to Lance Clayton.

Lance stood there with his thoughts racing, trying to keep his chagrin from showing. Tricked! Tricked by a two-faced dance-hall girl! Would he ever learn that women were not to be trusted?

He had had everything—freedom, evidence, vital information. Now he had nothing. If there was a way to get out of that room alive, he could not think of it. Yet he must! Otherwise he would fail more dismally, it seemed to him, than any man ever had failed before. Beth Holcomb would be kidnaped. His four partners would not know, might never learn, the thing he had learned by the accident of a jealous woman's fury.

For Lance was under no illusions. He could see no reason why McGee should not kill him. He wondered, in fact, why the gambler had not killed him at once. He would have had nothing but popular praise and three thousand dollars for it.

Flicker Evans fingered his guns and wet his tongue with his lips. "Want me to pop him off for you, Boss?" he asked.

"Not yet," McGee told him calmly. "I think we may find some use for him. Later—" his eyes widened, looked not quite sane—"I think I will have Monk crack a few of his bones before the end." His voice had a caress in it.

Monk Slade grinned, brought his arms up, flexed his muscles. Then he laughed again, like a man who has pleasant thoughts.

"Tie him to the chair," McGee said curtly.

THEY MADE a thorough job of it. They bound his hands behind his back and then with a single long rope they bound him round and round, lashing him to the chair, so that he could move neither hand nor foot. Lance's heart sank. He had flexed the muscles of his wrists, so that they could not be securely tied; it was impossible to so flex all his body. He was helpless.

He looked at the girl with slow bitterness. "Everybody has a price," he said quietly. "What some people won't do for money, they'll do for fear, won't they?"

The girl said nothing. Her face flushed a little.

Monk Slade gave a last jerk on the knots. "Aw, shut up!" he said cheerfully. He swung the back of his ape-like hand almost carelessly against Lance's mouth. The blow came with bruising force. It knocked the man and the chair over backwards. The back of Lance's head struck the floor with a crack that dazed him.

Monk Slade laughed. "He looks good like that," he remarked. "Reckon we better leave him that way?"

"His brains might leak out," McGee answered drily. "Set him up again, Monk."

Monk Slade did so. "I'm settin' you up in the other alley," he informed his captive, grinning. "I'll be back to finish the game."

Flicker Evans snickered. "You're goin' to be all spattered around like a ten-strike," he said, wetting his lips. "You sure we better wait, boss? What you keepin' him for?"

"Ever hear of baiting a trap?" McGee asked wolfishly. "If these fellows run true to form, the other four will be snooping around before long. We'll have a little party arranged for 'em."

They stuck a gag in Lance's mouth then and left him. He felt pretty sick. He had not only failed—he was going to be the means of getting his partners into trouble.

CHAPTER 11
A FIGHTING MAVERICK

WHEN BLAZE McARTHUR recovered from the crack Lance had given him with a six-gun, the impromptu posse which had swept out of town after the four Mavericks was already returning, unsuccessful. It had gotten dark. There was no use in casting around further for a trail which they had never really found.

The younger of McArthur's two deputies, Dick Bevan, shrugged despairingly. "Maybe you could have trailed 'em, Blaze. I couldn't. They just plain disappeared. No sign of 'em anywhere."

An older man, who had also been in the morning's posse, swore feelingly. "Never saw anything like it," he said. "Those devils are slicker than anybody I ever heard of. They're foxes, they are. Me, I'm layin' off 'em. I know when I'm outsmarted. Why they could kill all of us, any time they got a mind to!"

McArthur set his mouth grimly and said nothing. Now that the Five Mavericks had openly appeared, they had to be caught!

After some thought, the sheriff set off for the Holcomb ranch. He had not yet had a chance to talk to Beth about the morning's happenings. He wanted to know how it had happened that Lockjaw Johnson had been hiding inside the ranch-house. And, without entirely admitting it to himself, he wanted to know particularly what had happened between the girl and Saint McGee.

He found Beth Holcomb alone and cold of manner. She told him straight off that it was no business of his how Lockjaw came to be there. Then she went to the safe and took out the brown paper packet which she had found in McArthur's vest.

"I think this is yours," she said, coldly. "Have you any way to explain how you happened to have $10,000 of Uncle Fred's money in your pocket this morning?"

McArthur flushed. "I reckon that wouldn't be hard," he said angrily. "He gave it to me—that's how!"

"Do you expect people to believe that?" the girl asked.

McArthur stiffened. He stood for a moment in silence, then he asked, "How do you think I might have gotten it?"

The question caught the girl unprepared. In her heart she could not believe that Blaze McArthur had murdered their uncle, no matter how suspicious that money and the will might look. But his silence about having either the one or the other looked bad. She had not intended to be so cold or to accuse him so directly. But his manner when he questioned her about the Five Mavericks had angered her. Moreover, she suspected her involuntary coldness had been a mask to cover up the extent of her hurt at the possibility that Blaze might be guilty. Now, too late, she attempted to soften her tone.

"You must have some explanation, Blaze," she said. "Don't you see how bad it looks for you?"

McArthur's face was stony. He tossed the packet onto the table and strode from the room. "You'll think what you like," he said as he went out.

Beth Holcomb stared after him a moment, hesitated because of an impulse to run after him, and ended by dropping into a chair with her face in her hands. "Oh!" she said softly to herself, "Oh, Blaze!" and began to cry.

McArthur got half-way back to town before his feelings permitted any very clear thought. When they did, his mind began to work on a plan to capture the Five Mavericks. Beth Holcomb was evidently their dupe. Through her....

He slapped his thigh. "Now why didn't I think of that before?" he muttered, and set spurs to his horse. He wanted to get to Dick Bevan. Dick was still pretty much of a kid, but he could shoot. And the plan which Blaze McArthur had in mind included no mercy for the men he meant to trap.

It was a simple plan, but it might work. He intended merely to take up a position near the Holcomb ranch-house until either the Five Mavericks came to Beth Holcomb or she went to them. He would shoot on sight and trust to the first shots from ambush to cut down the odds to where he and Dick Bevan could handle them. Two of the Five Mavericks would die—anyway—no matter what happened to himself and his deputy.

He kept his horse at a steady gallop. He wanted to get Bevan and begin their vigil tonight. He would have liked to have had more men but the more men in the ambush party, the greater the risk of noise and of giving the trap away before they could take the Five by surprise. Two would have to do. And they could drop at least two Mavericks, maybe more, before it came to an open showdown.

McArthur smiled grimly. He hoped that one of the remaining Mavericks would be Lance Clayton. He owed Clayton a little debt for that crack on the jaw.

LANCE, AT that moment, was thinking hard of Blaze McArthur. He could not be sure that McArthur was not an accomplice of McGee's, but he was beginning to suspect that that was not so. Suppose he, Lance, could manage to get himself arrested? It would give him a chance to tell the sheriff what he knew. McArthur might not believe him, but he would be forced to set a trap for the men who were going to kidnap the girl. And if the trap succeeded, that should be proof enough that all of Lance's story was true. He hated like poison to appeal to the law, but it looked like the thing to do if he could manage it.

Suppose he could get his gag off and yell—what would happen then? He guessed grimly that McGee or one of his killers would get to him and shut his mouth for good before his cries would be effective. No, that was no good.

Still the idea stuck with him that he ought to get rid of his gag. If Doc and the others were to show up…. He began to inch himself over toward the dressing table. If he could tilt forward enough without falling, he might be able to rub the gag off on a corner of the table.

It was slow work, and when he got there he saw that he was going to have to tilt so far forward as to be in danger of slipping, face down on the floor. He got his mouth to the corner of the table finally and worked the gag loose. He was about to shove himself upright again when his eye fell on a bottle of eau de cologne which stood on the table, and a sudden idea came to him. The rope which bound him round came fairly high on his chest. If he could break that bottle, get a long enough piece of glass in his teeth, he might be able to saw the rope through.

Slowly, he worked himself into a position where his nose could hook over the top of the bottle, then he pulled it toward him. He was able to get the neck in his teeth and he worked himself back to where he could make the bottle hang over one side of the table. He began to waggle his head, tapping the bottle against the edge. It broke, just raggedly enough.

He pushed himself upright again and began to work at the rope, holding the bottle neck in his mouth and moving his head up and down in a sawing motion.

How long he worked at that, he never knew. It was an almost hopeless task and a dozen times he was about to give it up, but always he forced himself to go on. But as the minutes wore on, the rope, too, began to wear.

If only he had time enough…! He knew that his captors would be back before long. Or had they already ridden out to get Beth Holcomb? He thought that unlikely. It was still too early. No, he could expect somebody to look in on him before long. If he could, get free before they came….

And then, just as the last strand snapped and he felt the rope on the rest of his body loosen, the door to the main saloon opened and someone—it sounded like two men—started down the hall. Monk Slade and Flicker McGee. He knew it with a curious certainty. Perhaps he had a subconscious memory of how their footsteps had sounded before, for listening to them was exactly like seeing the men who made them.

He slipped his hands loose, tore the rope from him, and began frantically rubbing the circulation back into his numbed muscles. The steps came up to the door and stopped. The handle turned. Lance held his breath. If Monk Slade came in first, he was lost. Before he could handle that gorilla, those terrible flickering hands of Evans' would blast death into him.

The door swung back with a sharp, quick motion. Lance snatched it wide with his left hand, while his right snapped forward and landed flush on the weasel jaw of Flicker Evans. The little gunman's head snapped back as though his neck was broken. His knees sagged and he fell back against Monk Slade's reaching gun-hand. Lance drove forward, snapped a jolting left to Slade's eye. The gorilla man's head went back, lifting. Lance's right smashed home, full on the unprotected jaw—a blow with all the weight of his body back of it—a punch like the kick of a mule. Slade went back against the wall, his half-drawn gun falling to the floor.

Lance stooped for the gun and Slade's ankle caught him under the chin, straightening him up and sending him stumbling over Flicker's unconscious body, back into the room. He looked up, dazed not so much from the force of the kick but at receiving it at all. He had never before met a man who could be on his feet and kicking after taking a punch like that. The man's neck and jaw must be made of iron!

Deliberately, Slade kicked the gun, sending it spinning half a dozen yards away to the end of the corridor. "I don't need a gun for you," he said, grinning ferociously, and stepped in, closing the door behind him, and turning the key in the lock.

Lance let him have it, left and right to the face. The flash-splitting shock of those blows rocked Slade for a brief instant, but again it was Lance who gave back, twisting desperately to escape the outhrust grip of those ape-like arms. Instinctively, he knew that if Slade once got a grip of him he would be lost. The power in those huge arms and shoulders was sure death!

AGAIN HE struck with both hands, ripping at the other's eyes. Blood spurted from one of Slade's brows. He straightened, no longer grinning. Evidently, the ape-like killer had decided that his blind rushes were a mistake. He came in this time with his long arms flailing, a sluggish whirlwind of blows that had the force of twin pile-drivers behind them. Lance stepped inside and smashed—right and left to the stomach. The other grunted but he did not give. Instead, one of his great hands gripped Lance's shoulder. That was like being caught by a grappling hook, and it gave Lance his first knowledge of what it would really be like to be caught in that apeman's grip. Desperately, he uppercut, felt the grip loosen, wrenched himself free, leaped backwards.

And then, for the first time in Lance's life, cold fear gripped him. He had given everything he had, and it wasn't enough! Never before in his life had he met a man for whom he wasn't physically a match. There might be better boxers, but Lance Clayton stood six-foot-two in his stocking feet and had a body of rawhide and steel. He would have sworn that there wasn't a man on earth who could take his best punches and still stay upright.

"I'm goin' to take your heart out with my hands," Slade snarled, and rushed. This time Lance did not dare to step inside those flailing arms. He side-stepped, slashed with his left and let the other go by. He had seen that Slade's eyes were closing. If he could side-step and slash until the other was blind....

Slade turned, snarling. Blood ran now from a cut over the other eye. He cleared his vision with a hairy paw and came in again. But this time he came slowly, crouching, his arms spread out, trying to crowd Lance into a corner. Lance backed, feinted, watching him warily. Then he stepped in like a flash and struck again, right and left. Slade's reaching hand caught at his shirt. Lance, his throat suddenly dry, twisted away, side-stepping. But as he did so, his foot slipped and he fell to one knee. Slade's dripping blood had been a trap to catch the man who had drawn it!

Before he could get up his gorilla-like antagonist had seized him. They went to the floor together. Lance felt a great hand reach out and close about his wind-pipe, while the other arm, like an unbreakable band of steel clamped him to the squat, thick-set body.

Desperate, filled with an unreasoning, surging panic, he fought—twisting, slashing with his battered fists. But there was no getting those crushing fingers from his throat. He felt the blood rush to his eyes; giddiness filled him. Slade's horrible snarling ape-like face was a blur of indistinct crimson. It was the end.

One more trick only there was in his reeling brain. He let his body go suddenly limp. Instinctively, the other's grip loosened for an instant, and in that fraction of a second Lance put all his remaining, frantic strength into one great heave. He did not break free, for that implacable arm tightened again like a flash. But he had succeeded in putting six inches between his body and Slade's. Desperately, he fixed his blurred gaze on the side of Slade's stubble-covered jaw, a half inch from the point of the chin. Lance put everything he had into that one sledgelike blow; heard the crack of knuckles on bone. Slade grunted hard, and for an instant his arms relaxed.

Lance fought out of the loosened grip like a scared and furious bob-cat, rolled over and staggered to his feet. The other, despite the smashing shock of that blow, came up, too. A split second too late! While he was still on his knees; head bent, Lance raised on his toes and sent the full weight of his body into crashing his forearm down, clublike, on Slade's neck. He went down again, struggled once, but the paralyzing shock on that other nerve-center had done its work. Slade was down to stay.

Lance stared, scarcely able to believe his eyes. It didn't seem possible that Slade—Slade!—could be out. Slade was never out. How long had he been fighting Slade, he wondered. It seemed like a very long time. He had come to believe that nothing could really hurt Slade. The opening of the door to the main saloon and an uproar of voices brought him to himself. Gasping for breath, his hands numbed and his knuckles bleeding, he stooped and took the key from Slade's pocket. Voices came toward him from down the hall. He heard somebody say, "It's Flicker. Somebody's got him." And then Lance came out the door again like a young tornado!

The man nearest the door didn't know until sometime afterwards what had hit him. And, after that, not even Lance could have told what happened in the milling confusion of that lightning mêlée. He only knew that when he once broke through in the direction of the rear door, it was to find McGee, cold-eyed, backed up against the end of the corridor there, with a waiting six-gun in his hand. Lance saw the murder frozen in his eyes, ducked, plunged back into the crowd before McGee realized his purpose.

It caught the others off-guard, too, enabled him to break free. Before him was the door of the main room and the stairs. The rest of the crowd were swarming from the door. Lance yelled, "Look out! He went this way!" and went leaping up the stairs.

HE GOT to the top before anybody started up. The main upstairs hall had rows of doors opening on either side, and another corridor joining the middle of it.

Lance hadn't realized that McGee ran a sort of hotel in connection with his saloon. He raced to the other corridor, turned into it and followed it nearly to the end before he began to try doors. The second one he tried was unlocked. He slipped in, closed and locked it softly behind him.

The pursuit had gotten to the top of the stairs by then, but the foremost men paused when they came to the other corridor without seeing anything of their quarry.

"Try every room," someone shouted.

Lance had moved swiftly to the window. It gave on an alleyway running between the rear of the building and the main street. It was a good deal of a drop, but that was not what worried him. In a minute, somebody would have sense enough to go surging out the doors to surround the building. He'd probably just hit the ground in time to stop a lot of lead. He glanced upward, saw that the eave of the roof had a gutter around it.

McGee's voice cracked out in the corridor. "We've got him cut off here, men. Get down and surround the building quick! He'll be getting out of a window."

Lance moved swiftly to the bed, snatched up two blankets, knotted them together, tied one end to the bed and dropped the other out the window. Then he stood on the sill and jumped for the gutter, caught it. The metal sagged, creaked warningly under his weight, but held as he swung himself up. A second later he was flat on his stomach on the roof.

It was just in time, for as he flattened out men ran around the corner into the alley, guns in hand. They stood looking up, waiting for him to come out a window.

One of them saw the blanket hanging and yelled. Almost at once he heard the noise of the breaking lock of the room he had just quitted. The crowd trooped in and waited for the excitement to die down.

He crawled to the rear of the building noisily after a cautious second. He could hear them swearing and marveling.

"That's nerve for you—took time to make himself a rope."

"Got clean away, by gosh!"

"Not yet, he ain't! Get after him, boys—we'll pick him up somewhere in town!" On that theory the enthusiastic crowd took up the chase. Others went back to their drinking and gambling, pointing out that it was useless to try to find a man like that in the dark.

In a few minutes, the alley under Lance was clear, but there was plenty of movement on the main street and every moment or so some curious group wandered in to look over at the window from where he was supposed to have escaped. That escape was already in the process of becoming legendary.

Presently, Monk Slade came out the back door, unhitched a horse, mounted and sat waiting. Saint McGee came out a few minutes later. "Where's Flicker?" he demanded.

"Off huntin' Clayton," Monk grunted disgustedly. "The fool's crazy mad because the jasper hit him—once! By jimmy, if he'd hit him as often as he did *me,* he'd have something to think about."

McGee swore. "I'll give him something to think about when I see him," he promised. "Well, we can't wait on him. It's past time. Let's ride!"

The pair thudded off. Lance came to his knees, tense. He'd have to chance it now. He'd have to ride and ride hard, without waiting to find the others. He'd have to handle McGee and his bunch alone. Well, that could be done. Then he realized suddenly that he didn't have his guns. This time he did groan. Where in hell were Doc and the rest of them, anyway?

As though in answer to his question there came, from behind the shed where he had left his horse, the soft hoot of an owl, thrice repeated.

He did not wait to answer. He got hold of the gutter, swung down, and then dropped. He landed with his feet under him and pitched forward with enough force to knock the breath out of him.

He picked himself up and started for the shed. As he did so, he saw the dance-hall girl, Kate, standing in the rear door of the saloon, and thought bitterly, "Let her yell—it's too late now!"

Four dim, familiar figures waited for him behind the shed. He wasted no time in greetings. "We've got to ride," he snapped. "McGee's after Beth Holcomb—goin' to kidnap her!"

He jumped for his horse without waiting for an answer, led him out and got into the saddle.

Nobody asked for any explanations. Doc Grimson said, simply, "Ready? Let's go!"

A voice spoke from the corner of the shed. "Better take these, Lance," it said pertly.

Kate was standing there. She had his guns in her hands.

CHAPTER 12
LOCKJAW'S QUEST

"SORRY, LANCE," Doc Grimson said apologetically, as they rode. "We thought you'd be ridin' out to meet us and before we found out you weren't, half the town was pilin' along on our trail. Took some time to throw 'em off. What happened to you?"

Lance told him briefly. There was no time for detail. They had to ride hard if they were to reach the Holcomb ranch before McGee and his gang got there.

"What's your idea when we get to the ranch," Charlie Parr asked. "Know anythin' about how these fellers aim to go about it?"

"Not a thing," Lance answered. "I figure that the thing to do is to get word to Beth Holcomb to be watching herself, and then lay up somewheres and wait for the skunks to show. We don't want to get mixed up with those punchers of hers. They wouldn't believe anything we said—they'd just start shootin' on sight."

"How many'll be with McGee?" Flint Maddox asked.

"Dunno. Only four, maybe, includin' himself. One of his rattlers named Flicker Evans was left behind. There's always only five of 'em whenever they raid, so I figure that's all there is in the gang."

"Sounds reasonable," Doc Grimson admitted. "We ought to be able to let them get right up to the house and start in. Then we'll take 'em."

Lance said, "The damn skunks! If I'd only killed McGee when I had the chance!"

Lockjaw swore feelingly. "Don't talk about it. I had him just as pretty—" He broke off, grumbling. "Say," he asked a moment later. "What yuh suppose he wanted to kidnap Beth for, anyhow?

He couldn't get that IOU cashed thataway. Hell, all he wants is the money…?"

Charlie Parr groaned something about Lockjaw's thick skull, but a second later he put the same question to Doc.

"Easy to guess," said Doc. "That two-legged snake figures on marrying the girl—after he's taken her to his hideout. When he does, it'll mean that the IOU is good an' he can have the ranch, anyhow. He knows that Beth would be too ashamed to do anything or say anything after—after what he's planning…."

Lance cursed. "By God, and we was mad about the bunch who'd been masquerading as us! Well, we got somethin' real to get our dander up about now!"

They rode on in silence for a moment—a silence that was freighted with a slow-burning, deep anger; anger which could only be atoned by the blood of McGee and his bunch, each knew. Finally Lance said, "Who'll go warn the girl?"

Lockjaw said in a choked, hard voice, "I'll go. Let me, please, Doc!"

Doc Grimson chuckled. "All right, Lockjaw. That's your job,"

Nobody objected, for they all knew that no one could move more silently than the apparently awkward Lockjaw.

The rest of the ride was made in silence.

When they got near the ranch they proceeded more cautiously, circling, to get into the brush at the side of the house, where they left their horses. Then all five moved forward to a point about eighty yards from the building. From there, Lockjaw went on alone, while the others concealed themselves in the brush and lay silent.

From their position they could see the lighted windows of the living room and once they saw Beth Holcomb moving about. No one else was visible. The bunkhouse was at the rear and to the opposite side of the building, with the corral near it, but evidently the punchers had gone to sleep, for no light came from that direction.

For the first few minutes the silence was complete, then Lance stiffened, listening tensely. From the road leading to town he thought he heard a faint thud of hoofs. That surprised him. He had not expected McGee's crowd to come from that direction. But he was not certain whether that faint momentary thudding was not the result of his imagination and taut nerves. In any case, the sound had ceased almost at once.

A few minutes later Lockjaw returned, to report that he had seen Beth Holcomb. "She says she's goin' to rig up a dummy and put it in her bed," he announced admiringly. "She's smart, she is!"

Charlie Parr snorted faintly. "Sounds like a sick calf," he muttered under his breath.

The minutes passed without any sign of the kidnapers. Once a slight movement in the brush on the high ground behind them and to their right snapped them alert and tense, but a cursory investigation showed them nothing.

The living room in the ranch-house darkened and a light went on in an upper room. Beth Holcomb was evidently going to bed, or pretending to. Presently that light went out also and the house and grounds were in darkness.

The Five had noticed, however, that the roof of the side

veranda offered ready access to the girl's room and nobody doubted that the kidnapers would enter that way.

Minutes passed, hours, with no sign of McGee. They got cramped and weary. And then, without warning, silently, the ranch-house yard was full of moving shadows—shadows which congregated near the veranda by Beth Holcomb's window.

Lance's eyes widened. There must be nearly a dozen of them altogether! This wasn't going to be so easy as they had thought it would be. He cursed himself for not having found out from the girl, Kate, how many there were in the gang. Just because they operated usually in fives, in order to impersonate the Five Mavericks, had been no proof that there weren't more of them. LANCE FELT Doc Grimson's hand on his arm, signaling him to move forward. He began to crawl with the others, keeping low and moving silently. Behind him there was a brief rustling in the bushes—some small animal, maybe. He had no time to think about it. Two of the shadows in the ranch yard had become dim blots on the porch roof outside Beth's window.

Doc Grimson stood up suddenly, "Run in on 'em," he said, and broke into a trot.

And then the hair stood up on the back of Lance's head. A Colt blasted twice in rapid succession—loud as the voice of doom in that still night air. Flint Maddox grunted and lurched forward at the same instant that Lance became aware that the shots came, not from in front but from behind them!

He whirled, crouching, as flame stabbed again from the farther bushes. His Colts roared and rocked in instant response, driving lead toward the spot where the flame had spat.

125

Doc Grimson snapped, "Charlie and Flint take the rear; the rest keep on!"

Lance whirled back to see that the shadowy figures in the yard had spread out, were taking cover. Doc Grimson had opened the ball in that direction. He was running forward, now, crouching low, stopping to fire, zigzagging instantly away from the spot from which he fired. The old, familial night, fighting game. Gunman's tag with Death, in the dark. Lance laughed low in his throat, feeling the bucking guns grow warm in his hands, smelling the heavy odor of burnt powder in the air.

Three to a dozen in front—and how many behind? Flint had been hit—could Charlie hold them? No time to think. Get forward, someway, zigzagging. But Doc had stopped, forted up behind a pile of logs. The odds were too big to cross that cleared space under a dozen guns.

Vaguely, Lance was aware that the bunkhouse on the other side had erupted men. From the windows above Beth Holcomb's scream rang out. "They've got me—!" It broke off, muffled.

Lance cursed helplessly. A voice from the direction of the bunkhouse yelled, "They've got Beth! Let 'em have it!" And the night blossomed with new flame. A bullet ripped into the dirt by Lance. Another chugged at the log Doc Grimson had tossed him. A third seared the calf of Lance's leg. Grim-jawed, he thumbed his guns, saw a shadowy blotch get up from the ground in front and topple forward.

Then he became aware that McGee's gang were giving back, were fading out of sight. He got to his feet, guns flaming. Instantly, a hell of lead cracked around him, ripped at his clothes. Doc Grimson's voice snapped, "Quit shooting, boys—give back!"

He heard Lockjaw say stubbornly. "No, Doc…" and Doc's voice, low, peremptory. Then they were snaking back rapidly through the bushes while the guns of the Holcomb punchers stabbed orange, searching for them.

There was a sudden confused thud of hoofs from the front of the house. Somebody yelled, "They're ridin'—saddle up!" Then the five of them were racing back through the bushes for their own horses.

"Who in hell was behind us?" Lance panted, as they swung into the saddle.

"Dunno," Charlie Parr grunted. "There was only two of 'em. I got one and the other moved around toward the bunkhouse."

They shoved out at a dead run in the direction McGee's gang had taken. After a minute, Doc pulled up short, the rest with him. A beat of hoofs ahead was clear in the sudden silence. They flashed into a run again.

The third time they stopped, the hoof-beats ahead were clearer. Doc slackened pace.

Lockjaw said in an agonized voice, "Aw, Doc—ride 'em down! They've got her!"

Charlie Parr growled, "Keep your head, Lockjaw—you know better than that. If you kill that horse under you, you won't find another."

"They've got good broncs," Lance agreed soberly. He knew too well what you could do to a good horse by trying to make a stern chase a short one.

FLINT MADDOX was silent. Lance guessed he wasn't having too easy a time staying in the saddle, and rode close to him. "Where'd they get you, Flint?" he asked.

"In the side," Flint answered grunted. "It's not much."

Lance frowned. "Rib busted?"

"Cracked maybe."

"Don't you think you better pull out?"

"Hell, no!"

Lance shrugged, feeling worried. If a man rode with a broken rib he might puncture a lung—but a possibility like that wouldn't stop Flint, so it was no use talking about it.

The crowd ahead, to judge by the sounds, had settled to an alternate lope and trot. Accordingly they did the same. Lance wondered if the others wouldn't tell off a couple of men to drop back and try some dry-gulching but decided they wouldn't. They didn't know how many men were on their trail—it would be too risky. And no doubt they figured that, once in the badlands, they would be able to throw off any pursuit.

By luck, dawn broke before the badlands were reached. Galloping up over the top of a rise, the Mavericks had their first glimpse of the men they pursued. It was impossible at that moment to make out the individual figures, but as the light grew, Lance found that he could see them plainly. There were fourteen horses but only eleven of them were mounted, and of these, one carried a girl!

Four men must have gone down in that brief fight. Not bad shooting, Lance reflected with satisfaction. If the Holcomb punchers behind them hadn't spoiled the game, they'd have gotten more, and kept Beth Holcomb safe besides.

He became aware that the crowd in front had also seen their pursuers, for the pace increased and they began to draw away. They were crossing broken country now, rising and beginning to be cut deeply by ravines. It was terrain well-suited to ambush, and as the crowd in front angled off to the left, following a narrow gulch, Doc slackened the pace.

The floor of the gulch rose abruptly to a ridge. When they came out on top they saw that the ground sloped down into the bed of what must have been, in other ages, a vast inland sea. Now, however, it was no more than a great expanse of sand, through which sparse cactus, mesquite and greasewood struggled upward to meet the blasting sun.

McGee's crowd were crossing this flat expanse in a direct line and Lance saw that beyond it the badlands began in earnest. In those great upthrust masses of rock and earth, it would be possible to lose even the most trail-wise pursuers. It was now or never. They had to bring the lobo pack to bay before the flat land ended. Once beyond it, Beth Holcomb would be lost.

Lockjaw turned a pleading and harassed face on Doc Grimson. "We got to run 'em down, Doc."

Doc Grimson swore, shaking his head dubiously, but he drove down the slope to the level land at a gallop, nonetheless. It was not until their horses' hoofs bit into the soft sand that Lance realized what they were up against. All the animals, except his own stallion, had been hard-ridden that day.

Doc Grimson turned to Charlie Parr. "What do you say, Charlie?" he asked. "Shall we try it?"

The older man looked grave. "It's killin' work," he answered slowly, "but once they git into that hell's country across there, we ain't goin' to find 'em soon. Maybe we better try."

Flint Maddox, white-faced and grim, his shirt soaked in red, nodded. "If we can get 'em in rifle range," he agreed, "we'll force 'em to a showdown."

"What do you say, Lance?"

Lance looked at Charlie Parr before he answered and smiled significantly. He had seen Charlie looking at the sky and knew he had seen what Lance himself had seen. "Let's go!" he said briefly, and rammed in the hooks.

Not a man of them but was warmed by the burst of speed those magnificent horses found to meet their riders' need. It was unbelievable, the bottom and the legs they had—but still more unbelievable the heart, the sheer bone-bred courage, which drove them in the face of their exhaustion.

Lance let his stallion out, drew swiftly ahead, until Doc Grimson's crackling voice brought him up. "Keep with the rest of us, Lance!"

It was an order, that. Lance resented it, but he obeyed. The others' pace seemed enormously slow to him, yet, despite that, they were gaining steadily. If the horses held out, it would not be long before they were in rifle range.

AND THEN, without warning, disaster struck. To the right of them, half a mile away, a dun-colored wall got up, moved toward them with the speed of wind. Before it, little whirling dervishes of sand ran, spun high, dropped, lifted again. One of them got up at Lance's feet, struck him in a gusty, stinging rush, and then the world was suddenly blotted out in a raging blanket of driven sand. The stallion snorted and stopped, trembling, turning his back to the storm. Dimly, Lance could see that the others had done likewise. It was impossible to ride in that stinging, whirling, sifting nightmare.

Against the wind, against the muffling, yellow torrent, Doc Grimson's shout came faint. "Close in!" They obeyed. They made their horses lie down, backs to the wind and huddled in the shelter they made, bandannas over their mouths and noses to keep the dust-fine particles out of their throats and lungs. Even so, sand, sifted through. Sand filled their ears, stung their eyes, drove through their clothing, gritted on their skins. There was nothing in the universe but sand—drifting, whirling, driving in furious gusts—and the light of the sun was shut out. They lived in a dark, amber-colored hell through which the threat of death beat on angry, suffocating wings. And then they discovered suddenly that Lockjaw was gone!

His horse, they found, was still there, crouched with the others, but of its stolid-faced rider there was no sign whatever. They shouted, singly and all together, but there was no response. Doc Grimson fired his six-gun, with the same result.

Lance crawled to Lockjaw's horse and felt in the boot for his Winchester. It was gone. "Thought so," he muttered, and crawled back to shout his discovery to the others. Charlie Parr cursed bitterly. But there was nothing to do but wait until the storm was over and then be delayed looking for Lockjaw, if they, and Lockjaw, were still alive. That storm might last a half an hour. It might last for days. More than one man had been buried alive in such tornadoes of drifting sand.

Lance's instinctive understanding of Lockjaw's mental processes had been entirely accurate. It was very difficult to get an idea in or out of Lockjaw's head. In this instance, he was completely obsessed by the notion that the kidnapers of Beth Holcomb had to be overtaken. When the sandstorm stopped his over-driven horse completely, he raged against the delay for only a short moment. It was obviously impossible to get a horse to move in the face of that storm, therefore it would be necessary to move without the horse.

Another man, isolated in that whirling hell, would have merely wandered in circles until he gave out. But Lockjaw was possessed of that sixth sense of direction which some animals and a few, a very few, men possess in common. It is not a process of reasoning or memory, that sense. It is an instinct—an automatic process—like the sense of balance. It brings its possessors accurately, in a straight line, to the place they want to go. Lockjaw, without ever having reasoned about the thing concretely, knew nonetheless that he possessed the faculty of getting to his destination even blindly in that hell of blasting sand.

As to what he could hope to accomplish, once he had arrived, that was another matter. The group ahead would also have been stopped by the sandstorm. All Lockjaw had to do was to go up against nine or ten armed and desperate characters, polish them off and lead Beth Holcomb home!

He pulled his sombrero as far as possible over his eyes, stuck his head down like a charging bull, and staggered off against that tornado of lashing, raging sand. The sift of the particles into the openings of his clothing was so heavy as to actually weight him down and his skin felt raw and bleeding from the sand. So fierce was the whirlwind play of the wind that sand drifted in heavy piles over his feet in the mere interval between setting one down and picking it up again. And so intense was the concentration of particles in the air that breathing through the bandanna was a continued suffocation.

He stumbled on, blinded by the flying sand, deafened by the howl of the wind, weighted down and gasping like a fish out of water, but as true to his direction as a homing pigeon. Stumbled on blindly until his foot caught on some unseen obstacle and he plunged forward, falling. He had a momentary glimpse, as he fell, of a huddle of forms and of staring, astonished faces. Then something cracked down on his skull with a noise that seemed to burst his eardrums and what had been a chaos of dun-colored, hellish light became darkness and oblivion.

CHAPTER 13
MAVERICK COURAGE

BETH HOLCOMB, held prisoner in a badlands cabin, stared at the bound form of the man in the other corner of the room and shuddered. She had heard the group around the table talking about what they were going to do to this long-faced Lockjaw Johnson and, while she hadn't been altogether able to believe what they said, it had added to the turmoil of confusion and horror into which her mind had fallen as soon as she had been brought into this place.

When McGee and Monk Slade had ducked in upon her and gotten away with her the night before, she had been frightened, but the full horror of her situation had not dawned upon her until now. Seeing the hard, brutal faces grouped about the whisky bottle in the center of the rough pine table was different. It brought home the fact that these were the men who, masquerading under the sign of the Five Mavericks, had left a trail of blood and death behind them wherever they had struck, and that two, at least, among them were the actual murderers of her uncle.

And McGee's voice was still in her ears, cold, sardonic, with its threat of things which she dared not imagine but which seemed all the more terrifying for being vague.

"You'll marry me," he had sneered at her. "You'll marry me and be glad of the chance. You'll be begging me to lead you to a parson before long."

Meanwhile, he had left her tied up, putting her off in a smaller room with the still unconscious Lockjaw. She could still hear the men outside, guffawing, cursing, waiting for Lockjaw to regain consciousness. Beth wondered if he ever would. She remembered the lightning ferocity with which Saint McGee had brought his gun down on the stumbling man's head. It didn't seem possible to her that anyone could survive such a blow. Yet the big man's stertorous breathing assured her that he was still far from dead.

If only Doc Grimson and the others would manage to find

them! She kept clinging to that as a last hope, though her good sense told her that it was a slender one. For a moment, before the sandstorm, there had been a possibility.... Even afterwards there might have been some hope had it not been for a freak of the wind which had enabled McGee's crowd to travel while the Mavericks were still in the center of the disturbance. And Beth knew enough about that malpai country now to guess the trail to the outlaw hideout could not be followed by anyone who did not know it.

The big man in the corner stirred, groaned, opened uncomprehending eyes. Beth leaned forward, shaking her head and grimacing to admonish silence. Lockjaw stared, then memory appeared to come back to him and his face reddened with rage. He opened his mouth to speak, but the girl's warning look checked him. She motioned with her head toward the next room and the voices that came from it. He nodded, and after a moment began to roll over toward her. His hands and feet were bound but he managed, somehow, to roll silently. Beth marveled at it, seeing how awkward he looked.

"Keep quiet," she whispered. "They said they were going to do horrible things to you when you came to."

Lockjaw looked faintly contemptuous. "If I hadn't been blinded by that sand," he began, vaingloriously.

"Sh-h! not so loud," she cautioned frantically.

Lockjaw smiled tolerantly. "Where we at?" he asked in what he fondly believed to be a whisper.

"I don't know," the girl told him. "We turned into what

seemed a box canyon, but there was a way out of it, then a long trail, twisting around. It don't think I could ever find it again."

"Charlie'll find it," Lockjaw said.

"You think so?"

"Sure!"—scornfully. "T'ain't no trail Charlie cain't foller."

The words set a faint hope flickering in Beth's bosom. Her hands tied behind her back, tightened on the red bits of coral—remnants of her necklace. She did not want to drop those last few beads here, for fear McGee would notice and guess what she had done.

It had seemed to her utterly hopeless, dropping those tiny red bits, one by one along the trail. She had thought of it too late, for one thing. And for another, it had been necessary to drop them too far apart. No one, surely, would even see them, and the four Mavericks would have no reason to connect them with her. She had dropped them chiefly in the hope that Blaze McArthur might come on one. The necklace had been his gift to her—the tiny bits of coral might therefore have some significance to him.

Even if he did not find them in time to save her, she reflected sadly, they might mean to him that she had remembered him at the last and known that he was innocent. For Beth was determined that she would find a way to die before she submitted to Saint McGee.

"How come they got you?" Lockjaw demanded.

"I was foolish enough to hide in the clothes closet," Beth admitted. "McGee took it for the door into the hall, after the shooting began, and found me there."

"I'd ought to have stayed with you," Lockjaw grumbled.

The door opened suddenly and Monk Slade stood there, grinning.

"THOUGHT I heard that there sweet voice," he remarked with heavy sarcasm. "He's woke up, boss," he added over his shoulder.

McGee came to the door. He looked coldly at Lockjaw, then asked, "How'd you like to save your life, Johnson?"

Lockjaw snorted. "You don't have to bother about my life, skunk," he said. "You better figger on savin' your own."

Monk Slade kicked him briskly in the face. "Palaver more polite when the boss talks to you," he advised.

Lockjaw looked at him from a wooden countenance. "Kick again, pole-cat," he said. "You'll wish to God you had, before I git through with you."

Slade drew back his foot, willingly, to obey, but McGee stopped him. "Let's don't waste any time," he said brusquely. "Listen, you—unless you want to be tortured before you die, you'll do as I say. I want you to get up and write a note to your pardners. Just a little invitation to 'em to come up here. If you do it, we'll let you off. If you don't—"

"What's that you want me to do?"

"Write to your partners, saying that you're sending the note by a man in this gang who is on your side...." He smiled ironically. "You can say that it's a gentleman who doesn't approve of our having kidnaped Miss Holcomb. Then you'll give them directions how to get here."

Lockjaw wrinkled his forehead. "What you want 'em here

for?" Then his face cleared. "I got it! You'll be waitin' with your gang to dry-gulch 'em when they come along the trail, huh?" He lay quiet a moment as though turning the idea over in his mind. "And you want *me* to write the letter to bring 'em here!" he exclaimed. Suddenly he began to bellow with laughter.

Monk Slade looked as though he thought the prisoner had suddenly gone out of his head, but McGee, whose perceptions were quicker, frowned ominously. "Well?" he demanded.

"You ought to git into the theayter business," Lockjaw told him, grinning. "I seen a lot of them travelin' shows that wasn't as funny as you are."

"We'll see how funny you think it is," the gambler snarled. "Flicker, bring that candle."

Slade said pleadingly, "Just let me soften him up a little first, boss. It's been a long time since I had one like this to work on."

McGee hesitated, narrowed his eyes. "All right," he said indulgently. "Go ahead, but don't take too long."

Slade flipped out a pocket knife and began to saw at the rope which bound Lockjaw's ankles. "You shore are one beauty," he said, grinning at him tenderly. "I bet you can take a lot, can't you? I bet you're one tough hairpin."

The rope gave and he tore it off. "Just git up on your feet now," he said, "before I kick you up on 'em."

"You cut my hands loose," Lockjaw told him belligerently, "and you won't do much kickin'." As he spoke, he struggled to his knees, and got up painfully on stiffened ankles.

"Why, you wouldn't want to spoil my pretty face, would you?" Monk asked mincingly. "It's already had all it needs. Look it

138

over. Kind of swelled up and all different colors, ain't it? One of your partners did that. But that ain't nothin' to what your mug is goin' to look like. I'm goin' to make you look like the stars and stripes on a bad drunk. I'm goin' to set your nose where your ears are an' hang your ears up to dry."

"You yeller-bellied centipede," said Lockjaw mildly. "You talk too much."

"I talk too much, do I?" Slade demanded, grinning. He swung one of his long, ape-like powerful arms in an arc and drove it home against Lockjaw's mouth. It was a blow fit to shiver a barn door. It landed on Lockjaw's face with a sound like the thud of an ax and drove him staggering back against the wall.

Beth Holcomb screamed, sickened. Lockjaw shook his head to clear it. "Hell," he said contemptuously. "You don't know how to hit. Can't you do any better?"

"I told you he could take it!" Slade exclaimed delightedly, rubbing his hands together. "This is goin' to be more fun than I've had since the parson split his pants!"

He walked over to Lockjaw and drew back his arm for another blow. Leaning against the wall, Lockjaw let drive with a foot like the swing of a sledgehammer. Had the kick landed fairly, it would have finished Monk Slade then and there, but the latter saw it coming and jumped back almost in time. Lockjaw's heel hit him hard enough to hurt but it was not hard enough to disable.

What followed was not pretty. Lockjaw kicked as best he could, but he was almost helpless against the brutal rain of blows which knocked him down time and time again. Stubbornly, jeering, he got to his feet only to be knocked down. Beth Holcomb shut her eyes, physically unable to stand the sight any longer. But she opened them again, fascinated, despite herself, by the spectacle of this great, barrel-chested man who could stand up under such a beating and come back for more, defiant and scornful.

A moment came when Slade himself paused, arm-weary and winded.

"You ready to write?" he demanded, panting. His grin had subsided and his small eyes looked red and angry, but his voice had a note of uncertainty in it.

Lockjaw said through puffed lips, "You couldn't make me write anything, if you tried all night. Where I come from we tie ribbons on sissies like you!"

BETH HOLCOMB gasped, and from the doorway where the others had gathered there was an involuntary murmur of wonder and admiration. "Untie my hands," said Lockjaw belligerently, "an' I'll squeeze the yeller guts out of you, just like the toad-frog you are."

McGee interposed. "We're wasting time," he snapped. "Tie him up again."

That was done, though not without some difficulty.

"Take his shoes off," McGee directed, "and go to work on him, Flicker."

Flicker Evans wet his lips briefly with his tongue and sidled toward Lockjaw. His contorted half-face had a look of voluptuous pleasure on it. Beth Holcomb watched him with unbelieving horror, as he lit the candle and knelt by Lockjaw's bared feet. "Oh, you can't—you *can't!*" she cried involuntarily.

Saint McGee's lips curved in a thin smile. "You'll find out that we can do a lot of things *you* never thought of," he told her significantly.

Lockjaw said, "Don't you worry about me, Beth—ma'am. I can stand anything these skunks can think up."

Flicker Evans sneered and stuck the flame of the candle against the sole of Lockjaw's foot.

Beth Holcomb screamed again and again, beside herself, as the odor of burnt flesh slowly pervaded the room and Lockjaw's face set in a silent mask of agony. "Will you write?" Saint McGee asked, at length, his eyes cruel.

"Go to hell," Lockjaw clipped out between clenched teeth.

"Try the other foot, Flicker," the gambler suggested calmly. "May as well have a little variety."

Beth saw Lockjaw's big leg quiver briefly as the flame bit at the other foot, but there was no other movement, no sound. Only the great veins stood out on his forehead, the muscles of the big bull neck corded and the sweat bathed the bruised and swollen features until it ran in puddles on the floor. Then, mercifully for her, she fainted.

She never had any idea how long she was unconscious. When she came to again, Saint McGee was talking. "It feels better when it stops, doesn't it, Johnson?" he was saying softly. "I could put some ointment on those burns now that would almost stop the pain entirely. You'd be able to walk again in a few days. You'd be able to rest and sleep and eat and feel good. You're a good man, Johnson. You've shown that, and we're always looking for good men. You could have a place here and be well paid. All you have to do is write a few lines, telling your gang how to get here. What's wrong with that? Aren't they good enough to take care of themselves?"

"They're good enough to take care of you," Lockjaw said in a voice which was no more than a croak. "They're good enough to make you wish you'd never been born, you poor tinhorn crook."

"Then why not give them the chance?" McGee went on smoothly. "You don't have to be their wet-nurse. Why not live? If you keep on refusing, I'll just have you burnt to death. We're going to build a little fire on your chest now, Johnson. That doesn't feel so good. You may think you've felt something, but what you've felt isn't anything to when the fire on your chest begins to eat down on you. It's going to take you a long time to die, but you'll die all right. Don't be a fool. They wouldn't stand this for you."

"You're a liar," Lockjaw said. "You're a yeller-bellied liar, you...." The names he thought then to call Saint McGee were new to Beth's ears and shouldn't have been heard by any woman. But Beth Holcomb did more than forgive him; she thanked God that Lockjaw had been able to think of them!

Flicker Evans reached in his pocket and took out some shavings which he had there, prepared for this, and put a pile of them on Lockjaw's bared chest. It was just a little pile at first, but the pile of shavings he put on the floor beside him was plenty big enough.

"I'm goin' to keep feedin' it," he said, his twisted mouth lifting in the travesty of a green-toothed smile.

Lockjaw said in a voice so calm that Beth Holcomb couldn't believe it came from a man who had been so tortured, "I'm goin' to kill you, you sick little rat. The feller that hit me—him that looks like a poisoned monkey—I'm just goin' to beat him so he won't never be able to stand up to a man's hands again as long as he lives. And McGee—I'm leavin' him to Doc and Charlie. But you, you filthy little toad-stool, I'm goin' to crack your neck with my hands."

"It'll be in hell then," Flicker Evans snarled, and touched a match to the shavings.

BETH COULD tell when the fire began to eat down by the way Lockjaw's body moved. The great barrel chest squirmed and quivered; the enormous muscles strained, trying desperately to burst his bonds; the sweat of agony stood out on a face drained of color. Between the clenched teeth a groan burst out.

McGee's voice held a hint of triumph as he asked, "Ready to write, Johnson?"

"Go—to—hell, you…" said Lockjaw, and then his big body relaxed. He had lost consciousness. Even for him, the agony had at last been too much.

Beth Holcomb began to cry. She let her head fall forward on her chest and sobbed as she had never sobbed in her life before.

Vaguely she was aware that Saint McGee had motioned his men out of the room. When, presently, they came back, they were grinning. Monk Slade carried a pail of water which he threw over Lockjaw. After a second the tortured man groaned, and opened his eyes.

"Well, Johnson," McGee said, his eyes cruel, "you won't have to write that note, after all. Miss Holcomb is going to write it for us."

Beth Holcomb said quickly, "He's lying, Lockjaw. I never said…."

McGee laughed. "No, you never said," he mimicked, "but you will say, when you get a touch of the candle under your feet!"

Instinctively, Beth Holcomb shrank back, her face paling. It would be unbearable to be tortured like that. They couldn't—they wouldn't….

McGee laughed again, reading her thoughts. "Oh, yes, we will," he said. "So you might as well give in now."

Lockjaw began to curse in a hoarse, choked voice. Beth Holcomb set her mouth, her face pale. "I'll die first," she said deliberately.

"We'll see," McGee told her, his voice suddenly harsh. "Go to work, Flicker."

Flicker Evans moved toward Beth and began to take off one of her boots; Lockjaw lay and sweated. This was a problem he had not foreseen and did not know how to handle. Should he betray four such partners as he had, to keep one girl from being tortured?

Flicker Evans lit the candle. Lockjaw groaned and said, "Wait! I—I'll write it."

McGee snarled, "Brought you around, did it? I've a good mind to burn her anyway, until she agrees to write it."

Beth Holcomb protested, begged him not to give in, but he refused to listen to her. They untied his hands then and gave him pencil and paper.

His mind was racing as it had never raced before. He had to find some way to warn Charlie and the others that the letter was a fake—some way that the gang here would not see. But then he discovered that he was not to be allowed to write what he wanted—McGee dictated the letter to him. He dictated it the way Lockjaw would talk, leaving Lockjaw to write it down in his own hand and with his own spelling. Lockjaw's heart sank. There was no way—no way. If only one of the others had been there—somebody with brains, to help him out. He wasn't fit to handle a thing like this. And then, at the very end, because of the greatness of his need, Lockjaw's brain functioned.

"Got that?" McGee asked, as he dictated the last words.

Lockjaw wrote them down painfully and then nodded.

"All right. Now, sign it." And Lockjaw obeyed. He signed it with a flourish, "Lockjaw J. Johnson."

CHAPTER 14
RED WARNING

THE SANDSTORM had whirled its blasting way past the four Mavericks just in time to let them see McGee and his gang disappearing in the badlands. They marked the spot and then began to look around for Lockjaw. It took a lot of time and the search, of course, was fruitless. Eventually, they decided that they would have to go on without him. But when they reached the edge of the sand basin and began casting about for sign, they found discouragingly little of it. It was the worst possible country in which to find and follow a trail.

After a couple of hours of punishing work they were no farther toward their objective than they had been before. Charlie Parr wiped a sweating face with his bandanna and said, "We been tryin' to make haste too fast. We got to go back and start over."

"You think you can pick it out?" Doc Grimson asked soberly.

"There ain't no trail what cain't be follered," Charlie said shortly.

At that moment, a rock clattered down from the high ground above, and they saw that a piece of paper was tied to it.

As though released automatically from the same spring, Doc and Lance leapt for the arroyo sides, clambered up them, their guns out. But when they got to the top there was no sign of anybody.

They climbed down again. Charlie Parr had picked up the sheet of paper and was reading it, with Flint looking over his shoulder.

"It's from Lockjaw," Flint explained, with excitement in his tone. "He's tellin' us a way to get in to those skunks!"

Doc and Lance read the letter over Charlie's shoulder.

"It's Lockjaw's hand-writing all right," Lance said, beginning to share Flint's excitement. "It can't be a trap. They'd never get Lockjaw to write for 'em if it was."

Lance was fanning his six-gun at the spurts of
smoke that came from the rocks ahead.

Charlie Parr turned slowly, his eyes troubled. "Somethin' bad's happened," he announced slowly.

"What makes you say that, Charlie?" Doc Grimson asked quickly.

"It's like Lance says. Lockjaw wouldn't write a trap to us if thing's wasn't pretty bad, *and this letter is a trap.*"

"What makes you think so?"

Charlie Parr stabbed a horny finger at the signature, "Lockjaw J. Johnson."

"Mebbe you don't know it," he said, "but Lockjaw's real initial is 'O.' 'O,' for Obadiah. There ain't no 'J' in the middle of it anywhere."

Doc Grimson whistled softly. "You think he…?"

"I don't see nothin' else to think. He was tryin' to tell us somethin', and he couldn't find no way to do it, so he stuck a fake initial in his name, same as to say, 'This don't really come from me.'"

"I believe you're right, Charlie," Doc said softly. "I believe you're right."

"That'd be pretty smart for Lockjaw, wouldn't it?" Flint asked dubiously. "Maybe he just started to write 'Johnson' and forgot he had already put in the 'J.'"

"It's got a period after it," Doc Grimson pointed out. "No, I think Charlie's right. You get a man under enough pressure and he'll think up a trick that in the normal course of things he'd never think of."

"What I want to know," Charlie said grimly, "is what the pressure was. This writin' looks kind of shaky in places. You reckon those yeller hellions have…."

"Torture!" Doc Grimson breathed, almost too low to be heard.

Lance Clayton suddenly clenched his fists. "By God!" he swore, his eyes gone abruptly murderous. "If they've...."

"What are we goin' to do about *this?*" Charlie Parr growled, tapping the letter in his hand.

NOBODY FOUND an immediate answer to that. Then Lance Clayton snarled, "The directions will bring us to 'em. Let's follow 'em."

"Yeah," agreed Charlie Parr drily, "the directions will bring us to 'em—plenty!"

"We'll be walking into an ambush," Doc Grimson said thoughtfully, "—an ambush arranged by a man that's plenty smart, and that's backed up by nine or ten good guns."

"It won't be the same as if we wasn't on our guard," Lance argued.

Doc Grimson turned and looked ahead of them thoughtfully. It was bad country. The directions had said to follow this arroyo to a broad sand wash, then to turn right into a canyon where they'd see two chimney rocks overarching. He thought he foresaw what would happen. The dry-gulching would begin when they had gotten midway through some narrow pass—guns in front and then, suddenly, guns behind—without warning.

"It'll be murder, Flint," Doc stated curtly. "Some of us are bound to get it—maybe all of us."

"The trouble is," said Flint slowly, "I don't see any way to get to Lockjaw. Charlie might pick up the trail, but it would take

hours. We don't know what's happenin' up there. We might be too late. I'm for goin' ahead."

Doc Grimson shrugged, but his eyes were glowing with a sudden emotion. "May as well," he assented carelessly. "We'll try to give 'em a surprise."

Charlie Parr stood staring at the ground in front of him. His eyes had gone back to the thing he had been looking at before the letter rolled down to them.

"What do you say, Charlie?" Doc Grimson asked.

Charlie came and shook his head and looked up. "Oh! Hell, yes—we'll have to go on, I reckon."

His eyes returned to the object in his hand. It kept gnawing at his mind that the thing was someway important. It was just a little sliver of red—a stone of some kind, he guessed. One end of it was smooth, the other roughened, as though it had some kind of groove in it. If it was natural stone of the country, it was a new one on Charlie. Oh, well—no importance in it, anyway.

"Let's get goin," he said, shaking himself out of the abstraction.

They moved up the arroyo, eyes alert.

Every rock now, every fold in the ground, every hidden canyon entrance might hide sudden death. The brief glint of sunshine on a rifle barrel, the wraith of a movement behind some rock, caught at just the right instant, might mean the difference between being killed instantly and having a chance to do some fighting.

They rode with strained glances flickering from side to side—all except Charlie Parr. Charlie, grim-faced and thoughtful, rode with his eyes on the ground. He wasn't sure why. It was foolish….

Suddenly he pulled up and slid from the saddle. The others saw him pick up some small object from the ground and stare at it queerly.

Doc Grimson bent to look. The thing was a sliver of red, with a hole through the center of it. "The other must have busted in fallin'," Charlie muttered. "This here's a bead all right." He looked up at Doc. "What do you think, Doc—something some Injun dropped?"

Doc Grimson shook his head slowly. "That's coral," he said. "I never heard of the Indians here havin' any of it."

"Who'd have it, then."

Doc looked at him with his eyes narrowed. "A girl," he answered softly, "a girl would be wearing a coral necklace like that must have come from."

The bead had lain near the entrance of a small box canyon from which, it could be plainly seen from the arroyo, there was no exit. The walls rose sheer on all sides.

As though on impulse, Charlie Parr turned into this box canyon, leading his horse. "Hey," Flint, who had ridden ahead, called, "that ain't the way, Charlie?"

"Yeah," Charlie said, "I know."

Once inside the canyon, however, it seemed all the more certain that no one could get in or out of there, even on foot. BUT CHARLIE Parr had the minutely photographic eye of the old plainsman. Now that he was here, he thought he saw faint signs of the passage of horses.

He angled off in the direction in which these faint signs seemed to lead, and then his heart jumped. Before him, nearly hidden between two rocks was another one of the small red coral beads.

He went on swiftly in the same direction and found another bead. Then abruptly, with ridiculous ease, the secret of the box canyon opened up for him. What had looked like one of the cracks in the rock was in reality a part of the wall, set out, so as to make an entrance wide enough for the passage of a horse. From the direction of the arroyo, this outset was not visible as such. Inside the narrow passage he found another bead and the traces of horse's hoofs were clearer.

He motioned to the others, who came at a trot.

It took only a glance to show them the significance of what Charlie had found.

"By God, Charlie!" Lance exulted. "You've done it. They were trying to lead up another trail, to dry-gulch us without even takin' a chance on givin' their hideout away. They must have left Lockjaw and Beth in the hideout. "We'll be able to get to 'em while McGee and his gang are still waitin' to ambush us."

In single file, they pressed on, eagerly now. The passage out of the canyon led upward and then through a deep crack into a small arroyo which was raised well above the level of the surrounding canyons and bottom lands.

They moved as quietly as possible, but without taking too much care, unconscious that a watching eye had spotted them from the one piece of high ground from which the upper arroyo was visible.

McGEE HAD placed his ambush cleverly but to make assurance doubly sure he had placed Monk Slade on top of a great, upthrusting rock which commanded not only the approach to the ambush but that to the hideout. Now, Slade went scrambling down to bring the news that the four Mavericks had found the route to the hideout and were about to avoid the ambush entirely.

The gambler, cursing violently, moved fast then. The outlaw's hideout consisted of the one long, adobe building, made partly of boards set in a deep depression and surrounded on all sides by high, rock walls. There were only two entrances to the place, that which the four Mavericks were now approaching and another, almost as well concealed, on the opposite side, leading deeper into the badlands. It was toward this latter entrance that McGee led his men. From it, he planned hurriedly, he could cut down on the four Mavericks as they emerged into open space, and then rush those who escaped the first volley.

So confident was he of the success of this plan that he sent Monk Slade and another man by a circuitous route to the first entrance, to cut off the escape of the survivors by that route.

Unfortunately, for the complete success of this manoeuver, the four Mavericks had moved faster than he had estimated. They were already in the cleared space and riding for the adobe building when McGee and his crowd arrived at the other entrance. There was no time to get into position or to fire carefully.

The gambler, in the lead, threw up his carbine and sent a hasty shot toward the galloping figure—a shot which brought Flint Maddox's horse stumbling to his knees. Then, overwhelming response of six-gun lead sent McGee ducking for cover.

When he had found it and was in position to fire again, the Mavericks had dismounted in front of the building and Lance Clayton had launched himself at the door. The gambler's eyes narrowed in triumph. The door, as he expected, was locked, and behind it, ready to cut down the first man who entered, or to take the invaders from the rear, were the deadly guns of Flicker Evans.

Lance, after trying the handle of the door and finding it locked, jumped back and charged it, putting all his weight into his shoulder. But the first attempt convinced him that he was attempting the impossible. The door was too heavy to be broken in in that way. He shouted to Lockjaw to open it, knowing that the shout was useless, and then sought the first cover available against the hail of lead which ripped around him. Doc Grimson, Charlie and Flint had already done so, he observed.

The available cover was not much. Some rocks and a watering trough to one side did, however, give some protection. Doc Grimson and Flint were at the watering trough, one at each end. Lance took up his position not far from Charlie Parr, behind some rocks.

He saw that the body of one of the outlaws lay visible, and most obviously dead, in the entrance of the canyon wall, and as he watched another pitched forward into view, holding his lower abdomen between clutching hands. Even in the heat of the fight, an involuntary shudder went through him. That would be neither a nice wound nor a fast death!

Then Lance was fanning his six-guns at the spurts of smoke which came from the rocks ahead.

Neither he nor any of the others saw the door which had withstood his strength opened silently. A twisted, venomous half-face looked out, took in the situation and came out into the open. It was obvious that Flicker Evans intended to do no half-job of it. From his first position in the doorway, he could not see Doc and Flint behind the watering trough but he could hear their guns, and obviously he had decided to get them in view before he opened up.

McGee, in whom the madness of the born killer also lived, swore in admiration. Flicker meant to get two of them with his first two shots and then he would have the other two under his guns before they could take in the situation and turn to fire. "Keep shooting!" he directed his men in a low urgent voice. "But look out for Flicker!"

There was more in that than just a desire to protect a man who was about to give him the victory, there was real affection in it. This Flicker was evidently a subordinate to be cherished.

He saw the wiry, nervous gunman creep out, come to a halt when he located Doc Grimson and Flint. Then, deliberately, the two deadly guns in those quick, slender hands leveled, covering Lance and Charlie Parr.

McGee saw Flicker sight carefully at Lance but he saw something else besides—something that for a moment robbed him of the power of speech or thought. Out of the open door behind Flicker Evans a huge, disheveled figure crawled, got clumsily, agonizingly to its feet.

"Flicker! Behind you!" McGee cracked the warning out in a frantic voice. Too late! As the half-faced gunman turned his head to look back the big figure launched itself.

LANCE, HEARING the shout, looked over his shoulder, and for an instant he too lay still, frozen with astonishment. For Lockjaw was there—Lockjaw who had not answered his call—and Lockjaw had his big deadly hands around the neck of that gunman.

As he looked, Lockjaw jerked the wiry figure to him, his right hand closed over the narrow, distorted jaw and twisted once, sharply. Lance heard a popping sound. It sounded loud, that sound, and somehow horrible.

He watched as Lockjaw tossed the limp body from him as carelessly and reached down to pick up Flicker Evans' fallen guns.

The fire in front, which had been halted as men gazed on that sight, broke out again now, and Lance turned to the work in front of him. He thought, "We can start crawling back toward the door now—once inside they won't be able to touch us. Then we can go out the back way, get close to the wall and creep up close to them without their being able to shoot at us."

It was sound strategy, but it reckoned without Lockjaw. Lance was suddenly aware of the big man's figure lurching by him. He caught a glimpse of a tortured, almost unrecognizable face, with tears running down its cheeks; heard an oath sobbed out, then Lockjaw was past him, making at a staggering run for the entrance where McGee's crowd was holed up.

Lance did not know that Lockjaw was running on feet on which another man could not have stood for five seconds, but something in the big man's expression told him that it was no use yelling to him to come back. Instead, Lance got to his feet and joined the charge, his guns blazing as he ran.

He heard Doc Grimson's shouted, "At 'em!" and saw that the

others were on their feet. After that he wasn't conscious of much except the necessity of placing his shots.

It did not last long, that charge. There was no zigzagging this time, no stopping to aim and fire, just a straight dash at the mouth of those blazing guns.

A bullet took his sombrero from his head. Another plucked at his sleeve, like a twitching hand. He felt a third bite at his ribs. Out of the corner of his eye, he saw Flint Maddox go down, and struggle up again. Charlie Parr was spun off his feet, and got up cursing.

A crouching figure in front of Lance got up, his Colt leveled, eyes flaring wide—insanely. Lance's right gun roared. He felt the buck of it against his palm almost before his mind told him he had shot. McGee's hands clawed at the air in an odd sort of way, then he went forward on his face.

He saw that a couple of figures were fleeing up the passage and flung a shot after them and then, suddenly, incredibly, there was silence. Lance glanced around him bewildered. What happened to stop that hell of noise which had been in his ears for the last few minutes? But his eyes answered the question almost before his mind had asked it. The ground before him was full of figures in odd positions—twisted, limp, grotesque. And there at his side were Doc and Charlie and Flint and Lockjaw, all on their feet, all with smoking six-guns in their hands, all with the somewhat bewildered and reckless air of men who have been enormously busy and suddenly find themselves without anything to do.

Then Lockjaw sank to his knees, with a groan, his face pale.

Doc Grimson jumped for him, examined him a moment with a puzzled expression and then saw those sockless feet! His jaw ridged out, his hands clenched, and his luminous gray eyes were pools of murderous wrath.

The man who had been responsible for this was beyond the reach of human revenge. Frock-coated, twisted, somehow ridiculous, he lay with his face in the furrow of dirt it had ploughed up, not a man any more but the mere, lifeless caricature of one.

Lockjaw said in a painful voice, "Beth—untie her."

Lance ran to do that while the others carried the big man back to the adobe. He had just cut her bonds when his ear caught the sound of horses' hoofs—a lot of them—somewhere outside!

He ran to the door, dragging his guns as he did so, and then stopped, surprised and undecided. Out of the entrance, through which they had found their way to the hideout, rode a dozen or more men, at the head of them Blaze McArthur. They galloped toward the cabin.

Lance saw that Doc Grimson and Charlie Parr were standing relaxed, waiting for them. He understood that there was no longer any use in fighting Blaze McArthur. He could be explained to now.

But McArthur required no explanation. He flung himself from his horse and stuck out his hand to Doc Grimson. "I'll have to be askin' you to excuse me Doc," he said simply. "I been on the wrong trail."

Doc smiled, warmly. "You couldn't be blamed for it," he said.

"Appearances was pretty much against us. But how'd you find out; how'd you get here?"

"We followed your tracks to the edge of the sand-basin and then crossed over and started cutting for sign on this side. Didn't find much but heard the shootin'. Just as we was about to fog in this direction, this pair"—he gestured toward Monk Slade and the other—"come along and turned into that box canyon. We follered and caught up with 'em. The rest was easy. Sorry we didn't git here in time to help. Where's Beth?"

The girl came out of the building then and walked straight into McArthur's arms. "Oh, Blaze," she cried, "I'm so sorry."

McArthur held her close. "You wasn't to be blamed," he said huskily. "It looked bad."

Seeing the puzzled expression on the faces of the others, he explained, "Beth found ten thousand dollars of Uncle Fred's money in that vest, as well as the will," he said, and then, turning again to the girl: "You see, Beth, when Uncle Fred told me he was goin' to leave everything to you, he said—well, he said that he hoped that some day I'd be runnin' the ranch just the same. He give me that ten thousand to buy a spread of my own, so I could get to be a cattleman instead of just a sheriff and a gunman—thinkin' that one day you—we—might...."

"I wish he were here to see it," the girl said softly.

LOCKJAW HAD been staring at the pair with a mixture of befuddlement and chagrin on his big, battered features. Now he said, "Dang *me*," like a man waking from an amazing and unpleasant dream.

The girl looked at him in sudden remorse. "Oh, Lockjaw," she cried. "I forgot. I want to kiss you even before I kiss Blaze!"

Lockjaw stared, almost forgetting to respond when he felt the softness of Beth's arms around him and the quick pressure of her lips on his. For a moment afterwards he sat looking dazed, then a fatuous expression of happiness came over his face.

"Say!" he said aside to Lance, "I bet she likes me almost as good as him!"

Lance suppressed a smile and said, affectionately, "I bet so!"

Then Lockjaw heaved himself to his feet, setting his teeth to stand the sudden pain. "Turn that there ape loose," he said to the men who held Monk Slade. "I'm gonna show the spavined, bow-legged sissie somethin' about hittin'!"